boo thang

A Halloween Novella

rilzy adams

For Kai
Your patience knows no bounds. Lord knows, I test it. I'm forever grateful to you.

author's note

I hope you enjoy Piper and Zeke as much as I did bringing their story from my imagination to the page.

Please note that this novella contains detailed descriptions of sex on the page, so bear that in mind as you move forward.

Happy reading!

synopsis

For Piper James, the scariest thing about this Halloween is how badly she wants her best friend's little brother.

Piper's birthday plans go up in smoke when a series of unfortunate events leave her best friend, Angie, unable to travel to Mexico for the Halloween weekend they planned. Angie thinks she's found the perfect solution when her little brother, Zeke, offers to take her place but Piper disagrees. A weekend trip with Zeke is a disaster waiting to happen. It's the exact type of disaster she's been trying hard to avoid since a drunken kiss between them ignited sexual tension that begs to be explored. Piper cannot think of anything more stressful than spending her birthday weekend trying to resist Zeke. Once the dust settles, she realizes this might be the perfect solution after all. She and Zeke can spend the weekend getting each other out of their systems then return home and continue like nothing happened.

Zeke has been halfway in love with Piper since he was a teenager. He thought his desire for her was just leftover feelings from all those years of pining after his sister's best friend but the kiss they shared proved him wrong. His feelings are real… strong… and *very adult*. He cannot believe his luck when he offers to accompany Piper to Mexico for her birthday and she reluctantly accepts. He doesn't take her reluctance personally since he knows she's only skittish because of the attraction she's afraid to acknowledge. Zeke happily agrees when Piper suggests they spend the weekend exploring the sexual tension between them and calling it quits once they leave Mexico. Zeke wants more than a weekend fling, but Piper has been an unattainable dream for so long that he'll accept whatever she is willing to offer.

It's better to have her for a short time than never to have had her at all.

The trip is more than either of them bargained for and the harsh reality creeps in as the clock ticks down to their flight home: *can a weekend possibly be enough?*

one

. . .

THE LOW-GRADE THROBBING at the base of Piper James' skull that threatened to develop into a pounding headache was proof lying was a waste of time.

Piper's protests were loud and persistent, but her own body told the truth. She was stressed. Very stressed. Irritatingly stressed. But still, she rallied.

She shoved down the maelstrom of emotions she felt, choosing to cover them up with big smiles and self-deprecating jokes. She hoped her best friend, Angie, didn't look too far past the light airiness in her voice because she'd easily spot the tension there. So, she smiled wider and laughed harder. She'd perform the song and dance for her best friend because it would only add to Angie's guilt if she knew how stressed and frustrated Piper was with the turn of events. Guilt she had no business feeling but had been evident during every conversation they had over the last three days.

"Please stop torturing yourself, Ang. None of this is your fault."

Piper reached for the glass of Merlot she'd poured as soon as she got to the apartment but hadn't touched. Angie made a face and tried to change the position she'd been lying in for the last thirty minutes. She tried to hide it, but Piper could see the sharp winces of pain with each move she made. Piper placed her glass on the coffee table and picked up the fluffy pink blanket that had fallen to the ground while Angie tried to rearrange herself, revealing the cast on her left foot.

Piper's heart hurt for her friend. Being confined to mostly lying down would be hell on just about anyone, but Angie was the most active person she knew. She imagined each missed CrossFit session sapped a bit of Angie's life force. That was another reason why she hated that Angie was wasting her mental energy blaming herself for how their trip to Mexico was disintegrating before their eyes.

"Don't lie to me," Angie said, a touch of heat in her voice. "We've been planning this trip for months, and it crashed and burned when we were only four days out. Don't pretend you're not disappointed."

Piper sighed. Trying to force the lie through her mouth that she wasn't disappointed would be an insult to both her and Angie. What happened clearly sucked, and no amount of wide smiles and jokes would change that. "Two things can be true at once. I can be disappointed and still believe you shouldn't be hard on yourself. It isn't your fault," Piper said, hoping she put enough conviction in her voice. "It's nobody's fault."

A few seconds passed before she amended her statement. "Well, except for the cat, I guess."

Piper managed to keep her composure for just a few seconds before her lips started quivering. She hadn't expected the statement to be funny, but as soon as she said it, the absurdity of the entire situation came crashing down, and she could barely hold back her laughter. Luckily, she didn't need to because Angie caught her eye, and soon, they were both laughing until their chests heaved.

"You're so wrong for that," Angie said once she caught her breath. She wiped an errant tear with the hand that wasn't in a sling. "I'm probably going to have nightmares about that cat for the rest of my life."

"I don't blame you, even though I'm still confused as hell. I know you've explained already, but I can't wrap my head around how you went from trying to pet that cat to ending up falling down the stairs."

"He took one look at me and decided there was no way I was going to touch him, then in his haste to run away, he managed to get caught up in my dress, and...total and utter chaos."

Piper shook her head, wiping away the tears that streamed down her face. The story still sounded as unbelievable as it had when Angie's boyfriend, Tremaine, called her shortly after Angie had been taken to the hospital to let her know her best friend injured herself at his parents' house while trying to play with their cat, Finchly.

"Anyway, that's not why I called you over here," Angie said, voice sobering. "We need to talk about the trip. I know you've made up your mind to just go on your own, but that doesn't sit right with me."

"Well, babe, you're in no condition to be jetting to Mexico for a Halloween party weekend, and they are adamant that we won't get any money back. Not that I can blame them when you consider we were asking for a refund three days before the event started. I'm surprised they didn't sign off the email '*be for fucking real.*'"

"I get all that, but it won't be as fun if you're there by yourself."

"It'll be even less fun to lose my money. In *this economy*? Nah, I'm going and drinking my money's worth... Hell, yours too."

It wasn't even about the money. Well, not exclusively. Piper had been looking forward to the weekend getaway. Eli Stewart, the promoter putting on the weekend, had several nightclubs in New York and New Jersey that always promised a good time. This weekend trip seemed to strike a balance between partying and fun activities for those who enjoyed Halloween. Although most tended toward Christmas or Thanksgiving, Halloween was Piper's favorite holiday. She loved how it could be equal parts spooky and whimsical. She adored it all — the dressing up, getting scared, the decorations...*everything*. And she'd been very excited to spend the weekend living it up in Cabo with her best friend.

"It's your birthday trip, Piper! You can't spend your birthday alone," Angie argued. Piper tried to reassure her that, birthday or not, she'd be just fine, but she wasn't having any of it.

"I've been asking all the mutual friends we have that you can halfway stand if they want to go. I'd give them my package and they'd cover their airfare. Almost everybody had plans, so I asked Melanie." Angie made a face. "Can you believe her cheap ass wanted me to pay her airfare too? Said it would be a convenience fee for saving the day."

"Melanie?" Piper asked, shocked laughter spilling from her mouth. "Are you trying to fix the situation or torture me? You know me and Melanie barely get along on a good day. How did she even get to be on a list of people I can halfway stand?"

Angie chuckled. "I was desperate, okay? The point remains..."

"There is no point. And even if there was a semblance of a point, you lost it when you decided it was a good idea to try to trap me with Melanie over my birthday weekend. Girl, please stop. Devote this energy to getting better. I've already accepted this for what it is. I'll go on my own, have a grand ole time, and spam you with photos every day. That's as good of a plan as we'll ever come up with."

Piper was silent, waiting for Angie to continue the argument, but before her friend could say whatever was on her mind, they heard the apartment's front door open and close. A few seconds later, Angie's little brother, Zeke, rounded into the living room with a few paper bags in his hand.

Angie's face lit up at the sight of her brother while Piper's entire mind short-circuited. She pulled herself together enough to send him a brief wave and a forced smile that she hoped Angie wasn't paying too much attention to because if she did, she'd recognize the awkwardness and wonder what was up.

Piper wasn't sure how to deal with Zeke after they shared a drunken kiss at the tail end of a game night at his and Angie's parents' house a few months before. She'd expected to quickly forget the kiss, but as it turned out, her body still tingled with awareness whenever Zeke was around, even though several weeks had passed since her extremely foolish lapse in judgment. Her eyes flicked to his lips, imagining how firm they'd felt pressed against hers as he explored her mouth with slow, steady strokes of his tongue.

"Hey, Piper," he said, deep brown eyes trained on her with a small half-smile on his face that let her know he *knew* she was thinking of that kiss. "Long time no see."

His voice was light, but she could hear the slight censure there. *You've been avoiding me,* his eyes seemed to accuse. She gave him a tight smile. Of course she'd been avoiding him, and she'd *continue* to avoid him if she couldn't get her hormones under control.

She and Zeke didn't talk every day, but they always hung out every couple of months and often bonded over their love of sci-fi and fantasy books and TV shows. They could sustain hours and hours of conversation just off the back of *Doctor Who* analyses and brainstorming a more satisfying ending to *Warehouse 13* alone. Their message threads were filled with recommendations and reviews, the occasional jokes and life updates scattered throughout. She always looked forward to hearing from Zeke, but she'd left him on read for months now. Piper believed self-preservation was nature's first law, and she refused to put herself in a position where she had to explain to her childhood best friend how she managed to trip and land pussy-first on her baby brother's face.

"Nice to see you, Zee," she said, keeping her voice measured. He wrapped an arm around her waist and pulled her snug into his body for a hug that felt way too intimate and lasted a little too long. Piper glanced at Angie when Zeke finally pulled away, expecting to see her observing their interaction, but she found her best friend frowning at her phone.

"Maya was my last hope, but she has plans," she muttered. "I've depleted my list. I never thought it'd be so hard to sell an almost fully paid weekend to Mexico."

"Maybe I'm the problem," Piper teased, careful to take a seat on the furthest side of the couch from where Zeke sat.

His gaze flicked between her and Angie. "What's going on?"

Piper hated that the deep baritone of his voice felt like a caress against her cheek. She took a deep breath, pulling herself together before turning her body so she could face him directly. "Call your sister off me, please. She's trying to make me change my mind about something I've already decided, and all it's doing is creating tension when we could be eating food, watching trashy TV, and plotting payback for the cat who got her laid up with a sprained wrist and broken leg."

Angie scoffed. "I've ruined Piper's birthday trip and I'm just trying to make it right."

"By asking people I don't even fuck with like that to come

to Mexico with me? She asked Melanie, Zeke. *Melanie.* I'd rather be laid up on a couch with two broken legs than spend my birthday with Melanie."

Zeke cast a horrified glance at his sister. "Angie?"

"I was desperate, okay?" she said with a small chuckle. "I ruined things and I wanted to fix it."

"By trying to send her away with the girl both of you kicked out as your roommate when you almost beat her ass and snatched her weave out her head after she swiped your meal prep?"

Angie's face fell, no doubt remembering the incident Zeke was talking about. Angie had returned to the apartment she, Melanie and Piper shared to find that Melanie had, once again, taken her food from the fridge. This was despite having three emergency meetings to discuss the inappropriate behavior. Piper wasn't sure why that was Angie's final straw. It could've been she was tired of talking, or maybe it was because those last two servings of lasagna had been meant to take Angie through the all-night study session she had planned. Whatever it was, her best friend had snapped and suddenly seemed possessed by the spirit of Mike Tyson. Piper mostly managed to pull them apart without any damage to herself, but she couldn't say the same about Melanie's weave. To this day, she still wondered how the three of them managed to maintain any semblance of a friendship after that, although she figured the decision to no longer live together helped. The friendship, however, never went back to what it had been before those two disastrous years of living together when they realized how selfish and irritating Melanie could be.

"My heart was in the right place," Angie said softly. "I didn't want you to be alone."

Piper paused, trying to think of the best thing to say to put Angie's mind at ease. She'd just started to speak when Zeke

7

chimed in, and Piper regretted dragging him into the conversation.

"I think she's right, though. You shouldn't be celebrating your birthday alone. You'd have way more fun if you went with someone else."

"Thank you, Captain Obvious," Piper teased. "In case you haven't noticed, your sister isn't in any condition to take a trip, and I'd prefer to go alone than try to have fun with half the people she was trying to get to come with me."

There was a short beat of silence before Zeke flashed them a bright smile. It was a smile that both she and Angie were accustomed to seeing from him, disarming and charismatic, and he usually pulled it out right before he did or said something he knew might land him in trouble. She worked out what was going on a second before his smile widened as he said, "I'm not doing anything this weekend, and I'd be more than happy to make sure Piper has a good time."

two

. . .

ZEKE KNEW he was playing with fire when Piper's light brown eyes flashed with hot irritation. He didn't doubt she'd have tried to strangle him if she thought she could get away with it. She only settled for glaring because Angie would be suspicious if she was overtly hostile. Zeke knew Piper wouldn't want her to think too hard about what was causing tension between her best friend and her little brother.

He shouldn't have felt the flash of satisfaction that shot through him at the knowledge he riled her up, but he couldn't help it. The spark of anger that made her even more attractive to him beat the dead silence she'd been giving him for the last couple months. He wasn't sure what Piper hoped to accomplish with her glaring when all it was doing was make him want to kiss her golden-brown skin and watch the irritation in her eyes turn to passion. Zeke believed in always going after opportunities when they presented themselves. And this? This was the kind of opportunity that only came about once in a lifetime. The sequence of events leading to this were so wild that it honestly shouldn't have come about at all. He wasn't about to let the chance pass him by, so he ignored the looks

Piper leveled at him, her eyes narrowing with annoyance, and focused on his sister. Under normal circumstances, he was sure Angie would push back on his suggestion, but she was feeling just the right amount of desperation and guilt for her face to brighten with interest.

"That's a great idea, Zee!" Angie said, voice tinged with the first bit of excitement he'd heard since his arrival. She looked over at Piper, eagerness brimming in her eyes. "What do you think? I can't believe I didn't think about this! Not the answer being right under my nose all along. This works, doesn't it? It might be like taking your annoying little brother on vacation, but you and Zeke get along pretty good."

Zeke struggled to not react to his sister's commentary.

Your annoying little brother.

There was nothing sisterly about the way Piper kissed him back that one night when, bolstered by liquid courage, he leaned in to see if those plump lips truly felt as soft as they seemed. He'd taken his time, tilting his head toward her slowly enough to give her a chance to back away if he'd been reading the entire night through the lens of his longing for her instead of reality. She'd shocked him by leaning right into the kiss...soft, supple lips tenderly caressing his own, a small, sweet gasp allowing him to slip his tongue into her mouth and finally taste her sweetness. The moment seemed to transcend time, and everything ceased to exist except for the gentle feel of her lips moving against his, the softness of her curves pressed up against his body, and his dick, heavy with arousal...until a sudden loud sound from the living room forced them apart.

It was embarrassing how often his mind returned to that moment nearly four months ago, and even more embarrassing that his body responded each time. Even now, while Piper shot daggers at him with her eyes and his sister looked at him like she'd owe him for life, his blood simmered in his veins.

"I don't need your little brother taking time out of his schedule to celebrate my birthday with me because he's feeling sorry for *me* and *you*, Ang."

"You know better than to think I'd make this kind of offer out of pity," he said. "I'm being purely selfish here. A weekend in Mexico sounds way better than the office costume party I'm being forced to attend. In a way, you're doing me a favor too."

"This is perfect!" Angie laughed with so much damn excitement that Zeke could see the moment a war started within Piper. She wanted to say no, but the relief evident on Angie's face was hard to ignore.

After a few seconds, Piper forced a bright smile and turned to face Zeke with a look that let him know her performance was solely for Angie's benefit.

"It does sound amazing," she said, though her voice sounded like it was anything but. "I'll call Zeke later so we can settle on the details."

Annoyance continued to radiate off her in waves even after she allowed Angie to pull her into a conversation about how excited she was now Piper had someone to enjoy the weekend with. He was surprised that his sister, as perceptive as she usually was, didn't see through the façade Piper was putting on. Maybe at that point, she just didn't want to. Angie was so desperate to no longer feel personally responsible for ruining her best friend's birthday that Zeke was sure she was already making excuses to justify why Piper seemed less than thrilled.

He sat quietly as they ate and gossiped while half-watching some reality TV show that he couldn't understand no matter how hard he tried.

An hour later, Angie's boyfriend showed up, and both he

and Piper decided it was time for them to leave so his sister and Tremaine could have space.

Piper leaned over and hugged Angie, careful not to press on any of the sore spots on her body. He followed, planting a kiss on his older sister's forehead. "Get better soon. Let me know what else I can do to help."

Angie flashed him the widest smile. "You've given me peace of mind by volunteering to go with Piper, *and* you brought food. You're currently my favorite person in the world."

She turned to Piper. "I hope y'all keep me in the loop. I want to live vicariously through you."

It took another ten minutes before he and Piper finally saw themselves out of Angie's apartment. The door barely closed before she turned to him, temper blazing.

"What the hell is wrong with you?" she asked. "We can't go to Mexico together."

He arched an eyebrow. "We can't?"

"Zeke," she said. "You damn well know this isn't a good idea."

She was taut and angry, but Zeke knew she'd chosen anger because it was easier than facing what was really going on. He stepped a bit closer to Piper, the scent of jasmine that always clung to her tickling his nose. He inhaled slowly, allowing it to wash over him before he stepped even closer so he was all up in her space. Her sharp intake of breath told him all he needed to know.

"You don't think you'll have fun with me, Boo?" he asked, calling back to the nickname he'd given her when he was younger because he couldn't understand how a person could be born on Halloween and decided she was a ghost. "Or are you afraid we'll have too much fun?"

"This isn't a good idea," she repeated. "And you know exactly why. Angie is only okay with this because..."

"She thinks you see me as the little brother you never had and that I see you as a bonus sister when what I actually see when I look at you is a woman I want to bury myself so deeply in that I'll need a map to find my way out. A woman I want to taste, tease, and pull so much pleasure from that everything in her world will cease to exist except her nerves frantically trying to make sense of each touch, lick, bite..."

"Stop it, Zeke," she whispered, voice suddenly thick and hoarse. "None of that can happen."

But she wanted it. He could see the desire that pummeled him like a rogue wave reflected in her eyes. She hadn't even realized it, but she'd leaned into him, chin slightly tilted up as if she was inviting him to cover her lips with his and see if she really felt as good as he remembered.

"And none of it will...if you don't want it to. I'm perfectly capable of spending a weekend with you and keeping my hands to myself."

I've been doing it half my life, he thought sadly.

"I wasn't implying you'd be inappropriate with me."

"I didn't think you were, Boo," he said. "But it still needed to be said. Look, if you want me to go back in there and tell Ang I've just remembered I had plans, I will...but it'll have to be because you genuinely think you'll have a better time spending your birthday alone than with me. Tell me that and I won't come."

Her eyes met his — flashing with the irritation of defeat — but she didn't say the words. She *couldn't* say the words. He hadn't expected her to. Piper would fight her feelings, but she wouldn't outright lie about them.

"I'll be at the airport for five a.m.," was all she said before she turned and stalked to the elevator without saying goodbye.

Zeke made a sound in his throat as he watched her hips sway, her jeans hugging her ass like it had a point to prove. He couldn't wait to know how those cheeks felt in his palms because even if she was unwilling to accept it, he knew that this trip would let them finish what they'd started in that darkened hallway all those months before.

And Zeke couldn't wait.

three

. . .

PIPER SHOVED the last few packing cubes into her suitcase before she began making sure all her documents were ready. She'd been home for a few hours now and still felt restless. She couldn't get Zeke off her mind. She hated that she kept replaying the conversation they'd had while standing outside Angie's apartment, but even more the fact her body kept reacting to the memory. She'd never seen that side of Zeke before. The kiss they shared had caught them both by surprise, an opportunistic exploration of the small spark of attraction that flared the last two times they'd hung out together. An attraction she'd tried to swat away with memories of how annoying Zeke had been as a kid and the six years between them. Yet the deliberate images of the gangly twelve-year-old she tried to keep at the forefront of her mind were no defense against the sudden switch that flipped the night of his thirtieth birthday dinner when it hit her like lightning that Zeke was all grown up.

"Look at you not being a baby anymore," she'd teased, leaning in for a crushing hug that made her tingle in places hugs from Zeke never did before. Her sudden and unexpected awareness of how firm he felt against her body made her face go hot.

"I've been grown up," he whispered against the shell of her ear. "You're just now noticing."

She'd thought she'd heard something seductive in his voice...something that made her want to challenge him to show her how grown up he was. Instead, she forced herself to back out of his embrace and sought out his sister, just to remind herself that he was forbidden territory. It didn't stop her from stealing glances of him in his black jeans, a black Henley, and a thick gold chain around his neck that she wanted dangling in her face. She'd decided it was a temporary lapse in judgement and expected the strange new sensations she felt whenever Zeke was around to disappear as quickly as they came. But they didn't.

Then there was the game night, the darkened hallway, the laughter of everyone playing a board game in the living room floating in the air, and Zeke pulling her in for a hug that lasted way too long. There was her stepping back, yet standing too close, intoxicated from one too many glasses of wine but also the smell of him, the heat of him, her need for him. Then there was the kiss, memories of which often pushed her over the edge with her vibrator nestled deep inside her in the nights that followed.

But nothing...nothing prepared her for the determination in Zeke's eyes earlier that afternoon. The lust, the way she felt him undressing her in his mind and how her clit throbbed with the excitement of it. His words were straight, direct and full of promises she knew he would honor if she gave him the green light, and his intensity had her nipples pebbling and enough wetness pooling in the seat of her panties to let her know she'd severely underestimated the trouble she was in. Because Zeke *was* trouble. The worst kind of trouble. The kind of trouble that came with the promise of pleasure that would almost make the fallout a fair compromise.

Almost.

She couldn't believe she'd gone out of her way to avoid Zeke for the last few months only for this to happen. The thought of spending the next three nights with him, trying to fight the attraction she knew they both felt, was enough to trigger a pounding in her head. She pushed away the anxiety bubbling in her chest. He'd given her an out, and she hadn't accepted it because she couldn't bring herself to lie. And, if she was completely honest, there was a part of her — the wild, rebellious part — that wanted to be with him, consequences be damned. She focused her attention on trying to tuck that wild, rebellious part away so she didn't send a grenade through her and Angie's friendship.

She was still fighting a losing battle when her phone chimed with a new notification. Grateful for the distraction from her thoughts, she immediately reached for it and found she'd received an email from the airline confirming her upgrade from economy to business class.

She shook her head and smiled affectionately. Angie was something else. Piper pulled up her number and let it ring as she did one final check of her bags. Angie answered on the third ring, voice sounding groggy as hell.

"Did you upgrade my ticket and go directly to bed?" she asked with a chuckle.

A few beats passed before Angie responded, voice thick with sleep. "Girl, what are you talking about? I've been out like a light courtesy of my last dose of painkillers since about twenty minutes after you guys left. I'm happy you're heading to Mexico in style, but I think it's probably Zeke you should be saying thank you to. I forwarded him all the information so he could book himself on the same flight, so he has access to our reservation. Look at him already proving he was the best person to take this trip with you. He can be annoying, but he's always been very thoughtful. I'm sure this is going to be a birthday you'll never forget."

Yeah, Piper thought. *That's exactly what I'm afraid of.*

four

. . .

ZEKE STEPPED under the steaming spray of his shower and allowed himself to relax for the first time since leaving his sister's apartment earlier that afternoon. He would have been surprised by how much he managed to get done in a few short hours, but he firmly believed that everything was possible with the right motivation.

His thoughts returned to the image of Piper leaning into him, face turned up and full lips quivering in anticipation of him taking her mouth, and felt himself harden. Motivation? Zeke had that shit in spades. Still, what he had accomplished in the last few hours was impressive. He'd arranged a last-minute appointment with his barber, even though he'd seen him just the week before, to make sure he was lined up to his satisfaction, given his apologies to the coworkers he'd reluc-tantly agreed to attend their office Halloween party with, secured a Halloween costume since going as a generic vampire was no longer an option with how seriously Piper took Halloween, packed his bags, and booked his ticket to Mexico. Zeke was grateful Angie sent over Piper's booking informa-tion when she sent the weekend's itinerary so he could make sure they were on the same flight. He went one step further, booking them both into business class because Piper deserved to be spoiled and he planned on spending the entire weekend catering to her in whatever capacity she allowed him to.

Thinking of Piper was always a slippery slope, and it was a little bit concerning how quickly he went from wondering how excited she'd been when she got the upgrade notification to being caught up in the memory of how her lips felt moving against his and yearning to know just how good those lips would feel wrapped around his dick. Zeke didn't chase away the fantasy as he usually did. He let himself imagine her mouth, wet and hot, moving over his hardness as he fisted his hand through her hair and tried to hold onto any semblance of control. He wrapped his hand around his dick and stroked, imagining Piper sucking him hard, cheeks hollow with determination. Tightening his grip, he stroked faster, wondering whether she'd keep her eyes locked on him as she pleasured him. Would he see dampness in those light brown eyes as she brought him close to the edge? Zeke groaned softly when he started feeling the familiar tightening in his lower stomach and tension in his thighs as he stroked harder and faster until he was releasing his pleasure in spurts against his shower's tiles.

He rested his head against the tiled wall, waiting for his heart rate to return to normal. Zeke remembered a time when bringing himself to an orgasm to thoughts of Piper helped soothe the ache for weeks, but this barely took the edge off.

He finished his shower, tense as hell as he worried about what being so close to Piper and not being able to touch her would be like. Zeke wanted to believe this trip would be an opportunity to explore things between them, but he knew better than to treat it like an inevitability. The ball was and would always be in Piper's court, and should she decide she didn't want to see where things could go between them, he'd live with it…still making sure both he and Piper soaked up the most the trip had to offer. He wanted to make sure there was always excitement in her eyes and a smile on her face, even if he burned on the inside to ashes of unfulfilled lust.

He smiled, grimly acknowledging that this trip had the potential to be the sweetest hell, and just like she'd held a bit of his heart since he was fourteen, Piper held the fate of this trip in her hands.

Zeke was pulling on sweatpants when his phone started to ring. He'd hoped it was Piper calling, but it was his friend, Rayon, who'd probably just seen the message Zeke sent him. He waited a few seconds before he answered the call, knowing Rayon deciding to call him instead of texting back meant his friend was either very perplexed, ready to roast his ass…or both.

"I read the words in your message, and I understand those words individually," Rayon said as soon as Zeke answered the call. "But they don't make one lick of sense when I try putting them all together. Help a brother out. You're going where? For what? With whom? When? And most importantly…*how*?"

Zeke chuckled at the tone of Rayon's voice. "I'm headed to Mexico for the Halloween weekend with Boo," he said simply, as if this wasn't out of the ordinary. As if jetting off for a weekend with Piper was a part of his reality instead of his most fervent dream.

There was a brief pause before Rayon started laughing, cackling really. "Did you finally open the pack of edibles me and Delilah got you a couple months ago? I know the young people are saying that 'delulu is the solulu,' but the message you sent is giving the kind of delulu that had to come from a shit ton of drugs."

"Bruh, shut up," Zeke said, but he was laughing. "Be serious for once."

"You're telling me to be serious?" Rayon shot back. "You messaged me saying you're about to leave the country with the woman you've been pining for since you were a literal child who probably still sees you that way. So again...what kind of sorcery is this?"

That he was very sure Piper didn't still see him as a gangly, pimple-faced kid was on the tip of his tongue, but he bit it back because it would mean he'd have to tell Rayon about his and Piper's kiss. He'd thought of telling his best friend many times over the course of the last few months he kept the kiss close to his chest, but something stopped him every time. It felt precious and fragile, and he was afraid speaking it out loud would make it disappear. He still didn't want to talk about it now, so he let Rayon's statement go.

"Don't worry, I can't believe it either," Zeke said. "It's like the Universe has taken pity on my ass and conspired to get me everything I want."

He paused, remembering that the opportunity to go on this trip dropped into his lap because his sister fractured her leg and sprained her wrist.

"Okay," he said. "Considering how this trip came about, I should be a whole lot less giddy than I am now. But still..."

He gave Rayon a quick synopsis of the events that led him to this point.

"Damn," Rayon said. "Sad for the pain Angie is going through, but you're telling me all of this is down to a cat, your sister's clumsiness, and you being in the right place at the right time?"

Zeke thought about it briefly. "I think that about sums it up."

"And since Angie and Piper were planning on going together, they probably only got one room, right?"

"Yes."

A few seconds of pause. "Again…what kind of sorcery is this? This is either straight up witchcraft or you're the luckiest man on the planet."

Zeke chuckled. He sure as hell felt like the luckiest man alive. Unless, of course, the weekend ended up being one long exercise in the practice of restraint.

"This is no longer about you," Rayon said. "Right now, this is about every young man who's ever had a hopeless crush. This is for them. Please, Zeke, I beg of you — do not fumble this."

"Yo," Zeke said through baffled laughter. "I'm hanging up because you're doing too much."

He was still chuckling at Rayon's foolish behavior when his phone started ringing again. The laughter stopped abruptly when he realized it was Piper calling. His heart slammed hard against his chest, and Zeke shook his head at how predictably embarrassing he was where Piper was concerned.

"Hey, Boo. Calling to demand I cancel the trip?" he teased, although as soon as the words were out, he realized how afraid he was that she might be. That his question met silence didn't help his anxiety. Another few seconds passed before he heard her soft giggles, and damn if his heart didn't clench a bit.

"Had you sweating, huh?" she said, giggling even harder before she cleared her throat and added, "I just wanted to thank you for upgrading my ticket. You didn't have to do all that, but it was a nice surprise."

"It's only what you deserve," he said softly. "I intend to give you all the things you deserve on this trip."

He expected her to argue with him over the statement since the sexual undertones were clear as day, but she didn't.

"I'll see you tomorrow," she said instead. Zeke couldn't stop the wide smile from spreading across his face. He bit back the impulse to suggest they ride to the airport together. That she didn't protest his innuendo or tell him to chill was a positive sign that she might be looking forward to seeing where things could go on the trip, but he wouldn't push too hard. He would give her space. At least for tonight. Because as soon as those plane wheels went up, Zeke intended to be all up in Piper's face. And in *her*.

Or he would damn well die trying.

five

. . .

I INTEND *to give you all the things you deserve on this trip.*

Thirteen words. Those thirteen words, spoken so effort-
lessly in Zeke's deep baritone, destroyed Piper's last bit of
resistance. Not that her resistance had been particularly strong
in the first place, hanging on by a thread ridiculously frayed
and primed to snap at any given moment. Those thirteen
words were that moment. The promise laced in those words
was a warm caress that slid down her spine and brushed her
indecision away. In the end, the choice was easier to make than
Piper assumed it would be. She was going to spend the next
three days with her best friend's little brother in her guts.

She expected the guilt that came months before, as soon as
she pulled her lips from his and had to sit with the realization
that she'd enjoyed — *really enjoyed* — feeling Zeke's tongue
against hers while his hands gripped her ass and his erection
pressed against her thigh.

She expected the emotion to knock her down like a boul-
der, instantly forcing her to reassess the certainty she believed
she felt. It didn't show up the way she feared it would. She
only felt tiny tinges of guilt coughing up its last breath, losing

the battle against Piper's curiosity to know what Zeke thought she *deserved*.

She wondered what would happen once her curiosity was satisfied. Would guilt roar to life, accompanied by the insidious tendrils of shame?

Piper realized she didn't care. She would ignore the guilt and shame if they came. She'd made her decision and was prepared to stand ten toes on it. Mexico would be Mexico, and they'd get back to regularly scheduled programming once they returned home.

Piper couldn't believe how quickly all the tension seeped out of her once she made a firm decision. Picking up her phone, she opened her message thread with Zeke. She stared at it for a few seconds, contemplating if she should send the message she wanted to send.

"No time like the present," she murmured as her fingers moved over the keyboard. If she was going to stand ten toes on her decision, there was no need to be coy.

PIPER

What do you think I deserve, Zeke?

She'd been finishing up packing her handbag so the only thing she'd need to do in the morning was get herself together when she received an alert signaling a new message. Her heart raced as she navigated the app to open her thread with Zeke.

ZEKE

> You deserve this Universe and all the Universes yet to be discovered. But if you're talking about what you deserve this weekend, it's very simple. You deserve to be dicked down by a man who thinks galaxies could be created off the beauty of your smile. You deserve to be dicked down by somebody who adores you enough to be reverential but has lusted after you for so long that he can't help but be fucking nasty. And so that there's no room for misinterpretation... I am that man. I hope I cleared things up for you. See you tomorrow.

Piper didn't respond. She *couldn't* respond. Because what did she even say to something like that? Her heart pounded hard against her chest as she tried to remember the last time she'd come together with a man where the sex resembled anything *like that*. She stopped after a few seconds, ashamed to realize that she never had sex that was anything like that. Had she had good sex? Yes. Hot sex? Of course. She could barely fathom what Zeke described, but she felt the truth in his words. His body felt like heaven against hers, his kisses left her dizzy and breathless with desire, and he ignited an inner greed that surprised the hell out of her. The thought of being with Zeke in that way was just as scary as it was exhilarating.

Let me be the judge of that, she typed but couldn't press the send button. She erased it and tried to go for something coy but eventually deleted that too. She couldn't think of a single thing to say in response to what Zeke had so clearly laid out for her, so she went with the only thing that seemed to make the vaguest amount of sense.

PIPER

> See you in the morning.

six

. . .

HE SPOTTED her before she saw him. She was dragging a bright pink suitcase behind her through the relatively crowded airport, looking way too good in black leggings and a black sweatshirt.

Nobody has any right to be looking so damn fine so early in the morning, Zeke thought with a small smile as he continued observing Piper. Her straightened black hair was pulled on top of her head into a messy bun, leaving only a few tendrils framing her face. And what a fucking perfect face it was, from her thick, full lips and light brown oval eyes that truly seemed to be the window to her soul for how expressive they often were to the small stud that glittered on the left side of her nose. He was, as he'd been when he first met Piper, rendered speech-less. He noticed more than one man stealing glances at her ass as she walked by.

Zeke tossed the coffee he'd bought when he arrived at the airport about fifteen minutes earlier so he could try to wake up a bit more while he positioned himself where he'd see Piper as soon as she entered the terminal. And what a beautiful sight. He was half-awake and tired as hell, but his dick still found time to show appreciation for her. He willed his body to behave as he approached Piper, who was fiddling with her phone as she stood just outside the priority check-in queue.

"What a surprise to bump into you here," he teased, chuckling as he pulled her into a hug. He resisted the temptation to linger in the embrace so he could continue enjoying how lush she felt against him. She grinned and rolled her eyes playfully at his silliness.

"I was getting ready to message you to see if you were close enough for me to wait for you before I checked my bag and went through security."

"I've been here," he said, and laughed when she made a face. It was well-known that Zeke and being on time weren't exactly the best of friends. "I made a point to get here before you, and I'm glad I did. Had a decent spot where I was able to watch you walk through the airport, leaving people with broken necks as you went by."

Piper rolled her eyes and gave him a playful shove. "Whatever, Zee."

"You think I'm exaggerating?" he asked. "I think I heard this one old man's neck snap as he tried to get a good look at your ass. May he rest in peace, but I can't say I blame him. I understand it, and I feel immensely grateful."

He saw her debating whether she would take the bait and ask him to clarify his last statement. He hoped she would. Her response to what he planned to say would let him know if she was serious about the vibes she was on the night before.

The internal debate took a few seconds, but her curiosity won out in the end. She fixed those pretty ass eyes on him. "What exactly triggered gratitude in you?"

He let the question sit for a few seconds, maintaining eye contact so she could see the unabashed lust in his gaze. "I'm grateful because for the next couple days, I'm going to see that ass up close and personal. Around swimming pools, out party-ing, and if I'm lucky...while you're throwing it back on my dick."

He took it all in, the slight flash in her eyes and the way her lips parted while he waited for her response, more nervous than he'd ever admit that she might shoot down the sugges-tion that throwing her ass back at him could ever be a possibility.

His heart went into freefall when a small, seductive smile curved Piper's lips. She cleared her throat, and her voice was soft and clear when she spoke. "Those first two things are a given, but the third... You're gonna have to show me you'll be able to handle it."

She smiled at him again before turning and starting toward the priority check-in area with a bit more sway in her hips than she'd had before. Zeke chuckled and scrubbed his hand over his face. He knew all of that was for his benefit. He watched her walk away — thick thighs, fat ass, hips swaying — and didn't even try to control his body's visceral reaction to the woman he'd been halfway in love with for more than half his life. When she turned around, flashed him another cheeky smile, and asked why he was just standing there, his heart threatened to beat right out of his ribcage. Zeke knew that even though Piper was throwing caution to the wind for the weekend and offering him access to her sexually, she'd never be willing to give him a shot at what he really wanted.

The disappointment that rose in him was as sudden as it was overwhelming, but Zeke pushed it aside. There was no need to be greedy. Especially when the way things were playing out right now felt like they were ripped from fantasies he never expected to come true. He smiled. Maybe Rayon was right about all of this being an edible-induced dream after all.

When he caught up to Piper, slid his arm around her waist,

and pressed his lips softly against hers, he knew every moment of this was real. He pulled her into him when she sighed into his mouth and deepened the kiss for a few seconds before someone behind them cleared their throat and forced them back to the present. Yes, everything about this was real, and he wouldn't waste any time yearning for the things he couldn't have. He needed to spend every second savoring all the things he would.

seven

. . .

PIPER LOVED TO TRAVEL, but she hated flying. There was something about being stuck in a metal box flying at high altitudes when humans weren't supposed to be able to fly period that set her nerves on edge. Once the flight took off, there was absolutely nothing she could do but hope she arrived in one piece. She was still trying to talk herself down from the spiral her mind usually went on when the flight attendant came by, offering a warm towel, and took her order for her pre-flight drink.

"Make it something strong," she said with a smile she hoped hid the anxiety she felt. The tall woman with mahogany skin and a braided updo smiled at her with understanding and promised she'd get her something strong but easy. Zeke ordered a ginger ale, and when she caught his eye, she expected him to tease her about how anxious she was. He didn't. He just reached out, took the warm towel she'd just finished with, and put it on his tray table so he could hold her hand.

Her nerves were frayed for a different reason when he

started stroking the skin on the back of her hand with his thumb. Piper pulled her bottom lip through her teeth, trying to stop the small moan lodged in her throat from escaping through her mouth. She stole a glance at Zeke and saw his mouth had curved up into a knowing grin as he started tracing light circles on her hand. She couldn't stop her mind from wondering whether this was how he would play with her clit when he finally had her spread out for him. She breathed deeply, biting harder on her lips while she lost herself in imagining the feel of Zeke's fingers caressing, stroking, and eventually thrusting into the part of her that was desperate to make his acquaintance.

Her clit throbbed, pussy clenching as she imagined the things he'd whisper to her as he brought her to the edge of an orgasm. She squeezed her eyes shut just as she took notice of the change in the way Zeke was stroking her skin. Light strokes gave way to firm circles, then gentle scratches, and it hit her that as she sat there imagining how he'd play with her pussy, he was using his thumb and the back of her hand to show her *exactly* how he would. She couldn't stop the small sigh that spilled from her mouth as she rolled her hips forward slightly, trying to press her aching pussy against the seat, hoping it would ease the need she felt. The sharp shock of pleasure that ricocheted through her body as she pressed herself into the seat and tightened her lower abdomen had another soft moan spilling from her lips.

Zeke continued stroking her hand. Light touches, firm circles, and the small sting of him gently pinching her before he started again, the strokes longer and lighter, the circles quicker, and the pinches just a little bit harder while she clenched her pussy, pressing down into her seat as the first stirrings of what felt like an orgasm unfurled deep in her belly.

She gasped, louder than she'd intended to. The deepening pleasure of Zeke's fingers moving over her skin and the shock that she was about to climax off the back of Zeke rubbing *her hand* left her dizzy. Her eyes were squeezed shut, so she didn't realize he'd leaned into her until she felt his warm breath against her neck. She almost came right then.

He kissed the shell of her ear softly and said, "Come for me, Boo. Wet up those panties so that when we get to the hotel, I can spread those beautiful legs and clean up the mess you made."

Piper lost the fragile grip she had on control as his words sank into her mind.

"Fuck," she whispered softly just as the orgasm she'd been building toward rushed over her like a wave. The moan had barely left her mouth before Zeke covered her lips with his, kissing her hard until she gave up and moaned into his mouth until her body stopped trembling.

"Did you make a mess?" he asked with the wickedest glint in his eye when he broke the kiss.

She thought of how wet the seat of her panties was. "I did."

He smiled at her, and Piper's heart beat faster. Why was he so attractive?

He planted another soft kiss on her lips, and Piper was mildly embarrassed by how easily she leaned into him.

"That's my good girl," he whispered, sending her entire body back into a state of freefall before he casually turned to the flight attendant who'd returned not a second too soon, accepting his ginger ale and the rum and coke the woman had prepared for Piper.

"That should calm you right down," the woman said with a broad smile.

Piper smiled back at her and noticed Zeke with that same

shit-eating grin on his face he always had when he was about to be cheeky.

"The cocktail was a couple seconds too late," he said to the confused woman with a chuckle. "I've already handled her nerves."

eight

· · ·

THEY SAY no good deed goes unpunished, and Zeke sat with that thought during the nearly six-and-a-half-hour flight from JFK to Cabo San Lucas. He couldn't even try to hide the ego boost he felt as he watched Piper fall apart for him while the plane was still on the tarmac. He would never get over the sight of the well-satisfied smile she flashed him when she finally came down off her orgasmic high or how exhilarating it felt to cover his mouth with hers so that her moans didn't fill the business class cabin.

Her shoulders had been stiff and tense from the time they'd taken their seats on the plane, but the orgasm had drawn all that tension from her body. She only panicked briefly as the plane ascended, but once that passed, she settled into the flight, sipping on her cocktail and drawing him into conversation about an upcoming book by an author they both liked. He engaged in the conversation, offering up his own theories about how the seventh book in the epic fantasy series they'd been reading for the last couple of years would go, but it was hard to stay focused. How did he focus on whether the author had jumped the shark when all he could think about was the small quivers of Piper's beautiful, lush lips just as she was about to come? The memories made him hard and kept him hard, and it didn't matter how many times he tried to throw himself into the conversations they had during the flight, reading the book he'd brought with him, or troubleshooting a piece of code that had been bugging him for at least a week — he could not ignore how badly his body yearned for Piper's.

His body yearned through clearing immigration and customs.

His body yearned as they treated themselves to a shot of expensive tequila from the open-air bar right outside of the airport.

His body yearned as they found a taxi to drive them the nearly forty-five minutes to the resort.

His body yearned as they accepted the glasses of champagne the receptionist handed them while they waited to be checked in.

And his body fucking revolted when Piper asked the receptionist if there was any chance that the double queen room she'd originally booked could be exchanged for a room with a single king bed.

She'd looked back at him and smiled a smile that let him know she expected him to fulfil everything he promised, and that was when Zeke knew he'd managed to fly right past the warning zone into territory more dangerous than he could've ever imagined.

This woman was going to be the death of him.

And he would die with a smile on his face.

———

"I know they said this was a top-class hotel, but I didn't believe them," Piper commented a few minutes after they'd stepped into their room. Zeke agreed wholeheartedly. He figured the property would be beautiful from the photos on the website when he did cursory research into the event, but he'd lowkey believed the photos were outdated and the claims exaggerated because the event promised two parties, including a late-night pool party. He couldn't imagine the customers who paid for a property that seemed more suited to a relaxing spa getaway than a weekend party would be happy when partygoers descended on the hotel.

But the photos online had undersold how amazing the property was. Their room was gorgeous, large and airy with authentic teak floors instead of the simulated tiles he was accustomed to seeing in even some higher-end hotels. The four-poster bed boasted the softest-looking white sheets, and the bed bench was a deep blue velvet, which added one of the few pops of color to the room. There was a small sitting area tucked into the corner of the room with an armchair and a chaise. Leaning against the wall in that same corner was what might have been the largest freestanding mirror Zeke had ever seen. Piper immediately commented on how the mirror was going to be amazing for selfies and outfit shots, but Zeke had other things in mind.

Later for that, he reminded himself. He desperately wanted to lay her down on the bed and make good on the promise he made on the plane, but Zeke knew his desire for her had to take the backseat to making sure she really enjoyed her birthday weekend. That meant he was going to fight through the haze of want he felt when Piper bent over to take something out of her luggage and prepare for the Halloween trivia competition being held in the main conference room in about forty-five minutes that she was excited about. She'd spent almost their entire walk to the room explaining to him why she knew she was going to take the top prize. The plan was to have a small pit stop in the room so they could wash off their long day of travel before heading to the conference room, where he knew Piper would win the competition just as she said she would.

He walked out to the balcony that overlooked a large pool with the ocean in the distance and Cabo San Lucas' famous El Arco rock formation glittering in the sunshine. He couldn't get over how beautiful the place was, but as corny as it sounded, nothing compared to the beauty leaning against the balcony snapping a few photos with her phone. He watched her for a few moments before he stepped forward and hugged her from behind, smiling when she immediately sank into his embrace.

"This is gorgeous," she whispered, the excited note that had crept into her voice from the moment they arrived at the hotel still there.

He kissed the side of her head. "You sure are."

He could feel the vibration of her laughter against his chest, and Zeke wanted to hold her like that forever as they watched small boats sail close to the formation and the warm breeze tickled their skin. She turned in his arms so she could face him. "Thank you for coming with me."

He grinned. "Not after you were ready to throw hands when I suggested it."

"And I should've," she said with a small laugh. "I knew there was only one way this trip would end, and I was worried about Angie giving me the Melanie treatment if she ever found out."

He was about to tell her that they were all grown and even if Angie was uncomfortable with the idea of them being together at the start, she'd eventually get over it, but Piper tiptoed and planted a kiss against his lips before he could get the words out.

"I was really stressing over it," she continued. "But then I realized that Vegas isn't the only place where secrets can be buried. We can bury secrets in Cabo too. Angie won't ever have to find out."

"That's what's up?" he asked with a small smile. He knew he didn't hide his disappointment when confusion flashed across Piper's face. He kissed her lightly before she could ask the questions he saw dancing on her tongue. "I'm going to hop in the shower. Let Ang know we got here safely before she starts blowing up our phones."

He'd expected this. He was idealistic, not naïve. He knew Piper only gave in to her attraction for him because she planned to cut things off as soon as the weekend was over. Being aware of the reality didn't stop it from hurting, though, even if it made him feel foolish. He gave himself a pep talk while he stepped into the shower and allowed the very cold water to wash over him. He couldn't do a damn thing about this weekend being the only thing Piper was willing to offer, but he risked ruining everything if he got too into his feelings about a reality he couldn't change. He wouldn't jeopardize this moment. He was going to make every hour, every minute, and every second of this weekend count.

Their secret would remain in Cabo, but Zeke was going to make sure his touch remained branded against Piper's skin for the rest of her life.

nine

. . .

SHE'D SAID the wrong thing.

Piper didn't know exactly what changed the mood, but when Zeke smiled at her with all the sparkle gone from his eyes, she knew there was something in the word vomit that spilled from her mouth that he didn't like. Before she could ask him, though, he was kissing her in a way that made her heart clench in her chest and left her standing there so he could go get ready for the first event. Or, well, just away from her.

She was still trying to figure out what had gone wrong when Angie answered the video call, and Piper got lost in giving her best friend a rundown on the flight over and her first impressions of the hotel, showing her the view from the balcony.

"Oooh, that's beautiful. I'm verrry jealous," Angie said. "If the room is as beautiful as that view, I'm going to go cry into my Frosted Flakes."

"It's gorgeous and luxe," Piper confirmed as she walked from the balcony into the room. "I need to show you the mirror. I've never seen anything like it."

She was still going on about the mirror and the four-poster bed when Angie's confused voice came through the phone.

"Piper? Where did the other bed go?"

Her heart dropped somewhere to the floor. She hadn't panicked so hard since the time she lied to her parents about staying over with a friend one night when she was seventeen. The plan had been going well...until it wasn't, and she ended up running into her parents in the restaurant of the hotel she'd been sneakily staying with her then-boyfriend, Malcolm, because they were determined to take their relationship to the next level before he left for university. The perfect plan she'd had for losing her virginity that night crashed and burned faster than her and Malcolm's relationship had during the year of long distance.

She was feeling almost the way she felt when her father had taken one look at her, hand in hand with Malcolm, and asked, "What exactly are you doing here, lil' girl?"

Angie was not her parents, and she was not a little girl, but Piper still tried to think of a plausible lie. She might be grown as hell, but she wasn't about to tell her best friend she switched rooms because she planned to spend each night with her baby brother buried inside her.

"There was a mix-up, but it'll be sorted out. We're just here to get ready for the trivia event that sold me on this trip in the first place."

There was a small pause, but Angie eventually took the bait and abandoned the bed conversation, choosing to tease her about losing a partner well-versed in Halloween knowledge and gaining Zeke, who was ambivalent about Halloween at best.

Piper laughed. "I'm going to win, help or no help."

"Did you just call me useless?"

Her gaze moved from her phone to where Zeke stood at the entrance to the bathroom...completely naked.

"Zeke," she gasped, unable to stop her reaction to seeing him standing there with droplets glistening against his defined chest. Despite knowing better, her eyes continued trailing until they landed on his dick — thick, a few shades darker than his body, and bobbing in front of him like it was trying to say hello.

Damn.

She swallowed, envisioning wrapping her mouth around his thickness, but snapped out of it when she saw the teasing smile on his face. It was then she noticed he had a towel in his hand and realized he was intentionally trying to rattle her, knowing she was on the phone with his sister. He chuckled, grabbed something from his bag, and sauntered back into the bathroom, giving her a full display of his ass.

"Was that Zeke?" Angie asked after Piper had been silent for a beat too long. She blinked back into the conversation, hoping her voice sounded normal instead of drugged by lust.

"Yeah," she said. "He's just getting ready."

Angie chuckled. "Why do you sound like that? He's being annoying already, isn't he? Little brothers can't help but try to get on your nerves. I swear there's some contract they sign. Anyway, go ahead and get your fun started. Give Zeke a hug for me and remind him he promised to be on his best behavior."

"Sure thing," she murmured, disconnecting the call and staring blankly at the bathroom door.

Best behavior? Piper grinned. Zeke sold Angie lies as tall as the Empire State building unless his idea of best behavior involved being an absolute menace to her body and mind. Piper dropped her phone on the bed and sighed. Two close calls with Angie during a less-than-ten-minute conversation was wild.

She needed to get a grip before she told on herself to Angie before the weekend even properly began. Every thought flew from her mind when Zeke returned to the bedroom with his dick still swinging. He smiled at her in a way that let her know he knew how badly she wanted him.

"Shower's free," he said, teasing smile still plastered on his face.

Zeke had been playing dirty all day, and Piper was tired of him thinking he had the upper hand. He needed to be reminded that two could play that game.

She caught his gaze and held it as she hooked her thumbs into the sides of her leggings and pulled them down, discarding both the leggings and her panties on her floor. His jaw tightened and his Adam's apple bobbed as he swallowed...hard. Piper's mouth kicked up into a smile she couldn't help as she pulled her sweatshirt over her head and quickly unsnapped her bra. She let those fall too. She watched him looking at her, drinking her in, with a satisfied grin on her face as his eyes raked down her body. When his gaze returned to hers, she almost wilted under the heat she saw there.

"Oh my," she whispered when she glanced at his dick. She'd thought he was impressive before, but watching him grow hard made her wonder why she thought tempting him would be a good idea. Her cheeks were hot. Did she really need to attend the Halloween trivia? Was winning really that important when she seemed to have a prize right here? She could think of several ways to better spend the time, and all of them involved Zeke's dick.

"My eyes are up here," Zeke said. His cocky ass grin was that of a man who knew he was blessed in that department, and his swagger suggested he knew no woman left his bed unsatisfied. Piper bit the inside of her cheek. She didn't have to talk to any of his old work to know the reviews were good.

"The look on your face makes me want to spread you out on that bed and do the nastiest shit to you, but we need to leave soon if we're gonna make it to the trivia on time."

She managed to push through the overwhelming lust she felt to find a bit of sass. "Just say you're not up to the challenge and go."

He crossed the small space between them, gripping her chin with his hand and tilting it toward him. His grin was wolf-like: predatory and filled with danger.

"Don't tempt me, Boo," he said, voice low and thick. "I'm barely holding on to control as is."

He released her chin, trailing his index finger down the column of her neck to her breasts. He gently squeezed her right nipple before repeating the same action with her left. The throbbing in her lower region intensified as she arched herself into Zeke's hand while he continued teasing her nipples. Her breaths came fast, the sensations coursing through her body overwhelming even though he was barely touching her.

"You make me want to forget the promise I made to myself," he was saying, although his voice sounded more like he was talking to himself than to her. She moaned when he pinched her nipple, squeezing just a bit harder when he noticed her reaction.

"What promise?" she managed to get out, heart thumping wildly in her chest when Zeke pulled her into him and placed a kiss at the side of her mouth. She burned from the inside out from the feel of his warm skin pressed against hers and the heaviness of his dick poking against her stomach.

"That I was going to make sure you won your trivia night before I bring you back to this room and make you scream," he murmured against her lips. A few seconds passed before he spoke again. "Go get ready before I change my mind, Boo."

His lips finally found hers, kissing her until she was drowning in it. When he finally broke the kiss, he shook his head slowly. "I need to have a taste. Just a quick taste."

Piper's entire body went haywire. Her heart raced, her nipples ached, and her pussy throbbed, leaking wetness against her inner thighs. She wondered if he knew that anything he did to her would be quick. She couldn't imagine being able to tolerate more than the lightest touch before she exploded. She couldn't think of a single thing she wanted more than to feel Zeke's lips on her body, and she knew the desperation was heavy in her voice when she fixed her eyes on him and said, "Please."

ten

. . .

ZEKE HAD PLANNED on resisting Piper. He'd just wanted
to tease her a little bit, give her something to think about while
they were at the Halloween trivia event, but things took a
sharp left turn as soon as he touched her. Or perhaps a sharp
right turn, depending on how he looked at it.

He dropped a kiss on those pouty lips before he grabbed
the towel he'd dropped on the bed bench. Spreading it over
the velvet, he guided Piper to a seated position. The scent of
her arousal lingered in the air, making him painfully hard. His
mouth watered as he imagined just how soft she'd feel under
his tongue...just how sweet she'd taste.

Zeke dropped to his knees in front of Piper. The position
was fitting since she deserved to be worshipped. His heart
pounded so hard against his chest, he swore he could feel it in
his ears as he parted her knees.

Zeke cursed, soft and low. He couldn't begin to count the
number of times he'd fantasized about this moment...dreamed
about this moment...woken up during the night all bricked up
because his subconscious imagined doing this very thing. He'd

been hard before, but what he felt right now was on an entirely different level.

He brought his face close to the juncture between her thighs and just stayed there, inhaling her sweetness. Piper might have the prettiest pussy he'd ever seen, but he would be first to admit he was biased. Zeke wanted to devour her, but he refused to rush the moment. Instead, he placed light kisses on the inside of her thighs, enjoying how she squirmed whenever he got close to her beautiful lower lips which called to him like a siren song. She moaned when he finally covered her with his mouth, licking, sucking, drowning in the taste of her against his tongue. He tried to remind himself to savor this moment by slowly exploring her, but his body had an agenda of its own as he pulled her clit into his mouth and sucked gently until she was moaning even louder and trying to grind herself against his face. Zeke was captivated by the smell of her, the salty, sweet taste of her, how soft she felt against his lips and tongue. His desire to throw all caution to the wind and thrust his hard, aching dick into her and feel her warmth and wetness felt like desperation.

"I'm so close," she whimpered, holding his head and pulling him closer to her. He flattened his tongue and licked her clit with a firm, lazy rhythm. As Piper's moans got louder and her thighs began to shake, Zeke could feel his lower stomach tighten.

His dick was heavy and throbbing, desperate to be inside her...desperate to find a way to release the tension. He wanted to feel her pussy clenching against him as he came, but for now he'd take what he could get. He wrapped his dick up in the palm of his hand and stroked hard and fast as he continued devouring Piper's pussy, his body propelling even closer to an orgasm when she started gushing against him, grinding more forcefully against his mouth. Zeke could tell that she was close from those loud, hiccupping cries, so he kept up that same rhythm until she reached a crescendo, her entire body tensing a few seconds before she was throbbing and bucking against him as the evidence of her pleasure coated his tongue and mouth.

Zeke couldn't hold it back any longer. With barely two more pumps, his own orgasm came with him groaning hard against Piper's pussy, the vibration setting off another round of shaking and gushing from the beautiful woman spread out for him.

Zeke stayed there for a few seconds, dazed, satiated but still wanting more, before he pulled himself up from his knees and headed to the bathroom for a wet rag to clean himself and help Piper with the mess she made. After he finished running the warm, wet cloth over Piper's body, he helped her to her feet, checked his watch, and tapped her playfully on the ass. "We can still make it to Halloween trivia sort of on time if we hurry."

eleven

. . .

"THIS IS AMAZING," Piper breathed. She and Zeke had just stepped into the hotel's main conference room, surprisingly managing to be right on time.

She felt loose and relaxed as if her body was still trying to rearrange itself from the jelly it'd turned into after the orgasm she'd had. She'd been underwhelmed by the lack of Halloween décor when she'd first arrived at the hotel but pushed the disappointment away as she took in just how beautiful and luxe the property was.

She couldn't stop the broad smile from spreading on her face when she stepped into the conference room, though. Where the rest of the hotel lacked Halloween décor, the conference room was a perfectly arranged Halloween escape.

Several people milled around the large room, munching on snacks or drinking cocktails from the large tables set up throughout the room. The black and orange décor was understated with carved pumpkins placed around the four corners of the room, and elegant silver candelabras acted as centerpieces on each table, which were adorned with sparkly black tablecloths.

"I didn't expect this many people," Zeke whispered as they found a table in the middle of the room. She sat down and immediately reached for the snack tray, picking up a marshmallow stick decorated to look like a surprised ghost and taking a bite.

"I didn't expect so many people either," she said, genuinely surprised. She knew the event host was popular, but she hadn't realized he was *this* popular. No wonder the hotel hadn't minded having an event that might interrupt the ambience they curated… Most of the rooms booked were probably occupied by people attending the event.

The chatter died down when a woman in a black robe and a witch's hat appeared on the raised stage at the very end of the conference room. She took a seat next to the huge ass cauldron that sat center stage.

"Hello! I hope you guys had fun mingling, but we're now going to start the trivia portion of the event. Remember, there are prizes to be won! Organize yourselves into teams of four or five and we'll get started."

Piper flashed Zeke an apologetic look before turning in her chair so she could observe the other attendees. Some partygoers were already decked out in Halloween costumes, even though the costume party wasn't until Halloween night. She instinctively thought about teaming up with some of those people because they seemed to take Halloween as seriously as she did, even though she was just wearing a pair of faded blue shorts and a black tank top. She was about to tell Zeke about her strategy when she caught the eye of a Black woman with red locs that went down to her waist, dressed in the most vibrant green jumpsuit. The stranger smiled and nodded, and without any further conversation, she touched the elbow of the woman with her before they both meandered over to the table with broad smiles on their faces.

"I'm Georgetta, and this is my sister, Genae," the woman with the locs said, grabbing the empty chair next to Piper. Genae waved as she sat down and in an excited tone said, "Glad we could join you. I think my sister could take this trivia on her own, I'm just along for the ride."

Georgetta laughed. "I'm the one who's somehow obsessed with this holiday, and Genae is merely tolerating me. She surprised me with this weekend as a birthday present. I didn't even know things like this existed. I feel like a kid on the playground."

Genae chuckled. "Which of you is which?"

"I'm along for the ride," Zeke offered. "Boo is also a Halloween baby and has been obsessed with it for almost all the time I've known her. I don't even think I need to be here, honestly."

Piper playfully smacked him. "I'm not even all that bad."

Zeke raised an eyebrow, chuckling lightly before reaching out and tweaking her nose. "Okay, Pinocchio."

Genae's eyes bounced between them both. "Y'all cute. How long have you been dating?"

The denial rose to Piper's lips, but before she could set her straight, the host announced they were going to begin.

The next few hours passed in a flurry of good laughs and bursts of competitiveness from Georgetta and Piper that had Zeke and Genae sitting back and laughing.

Piper was able to answer that *Paranormal Activity 3* was the most successful movie of the franchise, that *The Conjuring 3: The Devil Made Me Do It* was based on the true story of Arne Cheyenne Johnson, and that the Disney movie *Hocus Pocus* was originally supposed to be called *Halloween House*. Georgetta knew that the Celtic holiday that Halloween originated from was called Samhain and that dressing up as a priest, nun, or clergy member could get a person slapped with a misdemeanor in Alabama. Zeke surprisingly came in clutch, naming Harry Houdini as the magician who died on Halloween.

"Just a lucky guess," he'd said with a smile that landed straight between her legs.

In the end, they took the overall prize and won spa certificates.

"Mission accomplished," Piper said with a huge smile, holding the envelope containing her and Zeke's couples massage certificate close to her chest. The four of them chatted a little while longer while servers came around with the signature drink — Black Magic sangrias — and other table snacks. The conversation was lively, but Piper couldn't get into it as much as she hoped...not when Zeke had his arm casually thrown across the back of her chair, occasionally stopping to rub her shoulder or run his fingertips across the back of her neck. Zeke had already brought her to two orgasms for the day, but Piper's body wasn't satiated, and she didn't think it would be until she finally felt him move deep inside her and pleasure became a mutual exchange between them.

She hovered at the edge of the conversation, trying to find an appropriate opening to feign exhaustion. She was still searching for that opening when Georgetta suggested they all go to the hotel's poolside bar to continue hanging out. A small smile crossed Genae's face, and that was when Piper knew she'd seen her flash of panic.

"I think these two have plans, sis," Genae said with a light chuckle. "But I'm sure we'll see them around before the week-end's done."

That a stranger could so easily see how badly she wanted Zeke should have been mortifying, but she didn't care. The only thing she was concerned about was how long it would take her and Zeke to leave the trivia event and get back to their room. Her patience had been running on fumes all day, and even those had evaporated.

"You're really feeling the kid, huh?" Zeke teased once they'd said their goodbyes to Georgetta and Genae and stepped out into the balmy night. He slid his hand into hers like they'd been walking hand in hand for their entire lives. It felt so natural...so comforting...so safe...that Piper internally scolded herself as they continued to the room.

She needed to remember what this weekend was supposed to be about and not get carried away thinking about how well they fit together. She didn't need to be caught up on how much she appreciated his sense of humor or the passion that always burned bright in his eyes when he spoke about mentoring a few kids at his old high school in programming because he appreciated how many opportunities being versed in STEM could provide. She didn't need to be focusing on how much they had in common and how easily they could move between the two passions they shared, reading fantasy books and travel. She shouldn't be thinking about how much better the trip she'd planned to Japan the next year to see the cherry blossoms would be if Zeke came along. And she sure as hell shouldn't have felt touched when Zeke told her he read his first fantasy novel at fifteen, a book she'd been raving about, because he'd wanted to be able to talk to her about it and then fell in love with the genre.

Zeke was only supposed to touch the places on her body that lit up like a fuse whenever he was near her. Her emotions were off-limits.

She couldn't think about how good they could go together. That slope was slippery as hell and would only end in tears.

twelve

. . .

INSECTS CHIRPING IN THE NIGHT, soft reggaeton music wafting from the pool area, and Zeke's heartbeat, which pounded like drums in his ear, were the only sounds that floated in the air as he and Piper made the walk back to their room.

Zeke stroked his thumb over Piper's hand, content to walk in the relative silence. He wondered if her mind was as serene as the beautiful look on her face or if her thoughts were like his, loud and chaotic.

Anticipation made him giddy.

Disbelief kept him grounded.

What would fulfilling nearly two decades of yearning look like...feel like?

Heaven.

He'd resigned himself to accepting that Piper would always be a misplaced crush that overstayed its welcome. That she would remain a longing deep in the marrow of his bones, but he would never know how *this* felt. Each time she'd glanced over at him during trivia with lust burning in her eyes, his gut twisted with impatience, but he'd forced himself to let the anticipation build. Some things were worth the wait, and Zeke knew Piper was going to be worth every second. He swiped his tongue across his lips and could almost taste traces of her sweetness.

Zeke was so lost in his thoughts that he was surprised by how quickly they made it back to the room. Something else hit him as Piper pressed her keycard to the door.

Nerves.

He shouldn't have been surprised by how his stomach flipped as they walked into the room or the small drops of precum already beading at the tip of his ridiculously hard dick.

Zeke wasn't sexually inexperienced. He knew how to plea-sure his women and was very confident in that fact. Whoever he brought to his bed experienced his single-minded determi-nation to please, even if things would never progress beyond a single encounter.

He knew how to leave a lover satisfied. But this was *Piper*.

He turned his attention to the woman sending his mind into a chaotic spiral, desperate to get out of his own head. She stood in the middle of their hotel room looking like every wet dream he'd ever had come to life.

He'd thought tasting her, having her under his tongue, feeling her gush into his mouth would lessen the urgency of the desire he felt for her. He'd been wrong. His desire was a beast roused from slumber, an animal turned rabid after its first whiff of blood.

"Are you gonna just stare?"

Piper's voice, soft and teasing, pulled him from the inces-sant thought – *fear* – that he could not live up to whatever expectations she had for him.

"I enjoy the sight," he said easily, coming to stand in front of her. He encircled her waist and pulled her into the hard planes of his chest. "It's a force of habit. I've been staring at you for nearly half my life."

He cringed, knowing he'd probably said too much. He waited for the vibe between them to turn awkward, but Piper simply smiled at him. His heart thumped hard against his chest, and his entire body went into freefall with that simple action.

"How do you do that?" she asked softly.

"Do what?"

"Make me feel like I'm the most beautiful woman in the world."

He chuckled, brushing his thumb against her cheek. "That's because you *are*."

He kissed her then, losing himself in the feel of her soft lips moving over his and the way her fingertips dug into his shoulders as she pressed herself against him. Zeke's nerves faded away. Nothing could coexist with the surge of need he felt for Piper and how perfectly she fit in his arms except the anticipation, yearning, and raw lust gnawing at his gut. He ignored the desire to guide Piper to the bed, undress her, and finally get close in the way he'd been wanting to for years. He wanted to take his time with her. He wanted to touch and tease and tantalize her until her nerve endings sang to the key of his desire. And as for him? He wanted to savor these moments like he would never experience them again because *that was* the most likely outcome.

He broke the kiss, running his lips along her jawline before he finally pulled away. The disappointment that immediately crept upon her face brought a tiny smile to his. He resisted the urge to kiss the pout from her lips, instead reaching for the control panel that sat on the nightstand to turn on all the lights in the room.

"I don't want a single inch of your beautiful body hidden from me tonight," he said, reaching for her hand.

Guiding her to the small sitting area, he pulled the chaise forward so they were almost close enough to touch the mirror that had captivated them both for entirely different reasons. He sat on the chaise and tugged Piper down gently so that she sat on him, her back pressed against his chest.

"I want you to see the way your body responds to me," he whispered against her neck. "And I want you to watch how well I know your pretty pussy will take my dick."

The small catch in her breath made his already hardened dick go even harder. She wanted him just as badly as he wanted her, and knowing that made Zeke want to combust from anticipation.

"Lift your hands up for me, baby," he said softly, tugging at the edges of her tank top as she followed his instruction. He pulled her top over her head and let it drop to the floor before making quick work of getting her out of the bra she wore. And…*damn*. He throbbed hard as he watched her full breasts in the mirror, her brown nipples already taut and puckered as if they were anxious for his lips.

Patience, he reminded himself as he gently teased her, playing with the hardened peaks while she squirmed against him. His other hand came to her waist to steady her because if she squirmed much more, Zeke knew all of this would be over before it began.

She was so fucking beautiful sitting there with her lips slightly parted, her breathing shallow, eyes closed as he gently tugged on her nipples, then a bit harder.

"Open your eyes, Boo," he whispered against the shell of her ear, satisfied when her eyes fluttered open. He watched her gaze fixate on him playing with her breasts — fingers teasing nipples, palms kneading and squeezing. She pulled her bottom lip through her teeth and moaned, the soft, sweet sound making him ache. He trailed his hands from her breast, caressing the smooth expanse of skin of her abdomen and moving lower and lower still. Her legs parted almost instinctively, giving him easy access. He wasted no time, fingers exploring her soft, wet heat. She moaned louder when his fingers found her clit and rubbed in firm, circular motions.

"Open your eyes for me, baby," he whispered again. This time, her eyes went straight to his hand between her legs. He slid a finger inside, enjoying the way she tightened against it before adding another and thrusting in and out until she was grinding against his palm. She was wet as fuck, so he knew his jeans were probably soaked. That made him even more excited to finally feel her wet and tight against his aching dick.

But first, he'd enjoy the utter contentment on her face while he watched her in the mirror. When she threw her head back and let out a keening cry as her pussy clamped his fingers tight, Zeke knew the image would be burned into his mind until the end of time.

thirteen

. . .

PIPER'S entire body was on fire. Through heavy-lidded eyes she watched herself in the mirror, chest heaving while Zeke took his time touching her — rubbing her clit, sliding along her slit, then gloriously thrusting his fingers into her as she felt the pleasure build in her belly. She continued watching the mirror, transfixed. He used his thumb to play with her clit as he continued thrusting inside her, and Piper gave up trying to fight the wave that was about to crash over her.

She came with a loud, sharp cry, and when Zeke kissed her cheek and started nibbling on her earlobe, her body jerked with aftershocks from the orgasm.

She couldn't think. Logical thoughts were hazy and far away as Zeke continued gently touching her skin. A glide across her shoulders. A small tweak of her nipples, lightly squeezing her breasts. Fingers circling her belly button. A barely-there brush against her pubic bone. Then finally, stroking her core, which still pulsed with need for him. She wasn't sure what she expected sex with Zeke to be like, but she hadn't expected *this*. She hadn't expected *him*. Just like she hadn't expected how incredibly erotic it would be to watch their reflections in the mirror. To watch his fingers trail across her body and slide between her legs and see the spark of satisfaction in his eyes while he watched her watching him please her.

She turned her face, tilting her head back so she could capture Zeke's mouth with hers. She kissed him with the passion she felt, struggling to get as close to him as their awkward positioning would allow as his hand came behind her head so he could pull her into the kiss. Then they became a blur of lips moving frantically, tongues lashing and her fingers digging into his broad shoulders. She was breathing hard when she finally pulled away and gestured to all the clothes he still wore.

"We've found ourselves in a very inequitable situation."

Zeke chuckled. His laughter, sexy and deep, sent another rush of pleasure through her body.

He kissed her briefly. "Let me level the playing field."

He got rid of his shirt first, and Piper wasted no time running her hands along the hard planes of his chest and stomach. Her heart thudded hard against her chest as her hands made their way lower and lower still. She'd intended to play things cooler than this. Even though she already knew this weekend would be about exploring the attraction that had blossomed between them, she hadn't expected things to be like live wire, always a few seconds from detonation. She hadn't expected her lust for him to be so visceral that a stranger could read it all over her body language. She *definitely* didn't expect her want to be so potent that her body was already moving to the floor, waiting for him to discard his sweatpants, which were the only thing standing between her and what she wanted — no, *needed* — most of all.

His smirk was cocky, but he'd earned being smug. He'd given her three powerful orgasms and she hadn't even gotten up close and personal with his dick yet. She expected him to make her wait for it, but Zeke didn't. He got his sweatpants off in one smooth motion and finally, she was kneeling there with an eyeful of his dick. Thick, dark, veiny...and a mouthful. She was looking forward to that.

"Are you gonna just stare?" he asked, lips quirking upwards.

She threw back her head and laughed at his tossing her own words back in her face.

"I enjoy the sight," she said, his little chuckle hitting her right in the pussy. She moved her body forward until she was between his spread legs. Bending her head, she ran her tongue lightly over the tip of his dick.

Satisfaction bloomed inside her when he inhaled sharply, so she took him into her mouth, meeting his eyes as she pleasured him. The intensity she saw in his brown eyes should have terrified her, but instead it spurred her to suck harder and deeper, until she could feel him tickling her throat. Then she sucked even more, wrapping her hand around the base of his dick and stroking in tandem with her mouth. She loved that Zeke didn't try to tone down his reactions to the enthusiastic, sloppy head she was giving him. Those sharp intakes of breath, groans, and damn well near moans got Piper even wetter, which was saying a lot because she was already dripping. When he wrapped his hands in her hair and told her how good her mouth felt on his dick, how he could barely handle it, and begged her to keep doing it *just like that*, Piper allowed herself the brief zing of gratification that she had the ability to affect him too. And when mid-groan, voice thick and deep, he demanded she *gag on his dick*, she happily obliged. She went at it as if she owed him something, taking him as far down her throat as she could, stroking him in a firm, quick motion as those groans became louder and more erratic...until he was trying to pull her off him. That only made her want to go harder.

"Ease up, Boo," he groaned. "I need to be inside you."

She was conflicted, knowing how much she was enjoying seeing him teeter on the edge of control but equally aware she was dying for him to be inside her too.

In the end, she allowed him to help her off the floor, straddled him, and kissed him hard while he rubbed her back.

"I can't wait any more," he whispered against her cheek. "Turn around, baby. I want you to watch yourself take me."

He said that roughly, and Piper's body throbbed in anticipation. His touches, no matter how light, inched her body closer and closer to combustion. The light pressure of his fingertips digging into her hips as he helped her turn around so her back pressed against his chest had her breath catching in her throat. She lifted herself off him and sighed when she felt his hardness pressed up against her entrance. Everything in the world ceased to exist except for her panting breaths and Zeke's small groan.

"Give me two seconds to get this condom on."

He pressed himself against her entrance for a brief moment before she eased off him to make that process easier. She wanted to be reckless and tell him fuck the barrier, but they were being reckless enough as it was. So she waited, the brief minute feeling so much longer as he ripped open the packet and sheathed himself.

"Come here," he whispered. Piper didn't need to be told twice. She moved back to his lap and lifted herself so she hovered over his dick. One hand splayed across her stomach, pressing her against his chest while his other hand rubbed her clit as his dick pressed lightly against her slit. Piper couldn't drag her eyes away from their reflection in the mirror and watched, transfixed, as her lower lips spread to let Zeke's dick inside. She moaned as she stretched to accommodate his girth, relishing the feel of being filled in the place where she'd been aching for him all night. Her eyes met his in the mirror and she clenched around him — *hard.*

Zeke's hands massaged her breasts while he ran his lips across her cheek before he whispered, "Ride for me."

Piper pulled her attention from the mirror so she could kiss him thoroughly, tugging at his bottom lip before she flashed him a smile. Then she rocked back and forth a few times before she lifted herself up and slammed back down on him, rolling her hips in small, tight circles before she repeated the motion again. His fingers dug into her thighs and twisted her nipples while she rode him, only the sounds of their skin slapping together and their cries filling the air. She slowed when she felt herself cresting the edge of an orgasm, eyes fixated on the wanton sight in the mirror of his dick disappearing deep inside her each time she moved. Of the deep lust in his eyes as he stared at their reflections even as his hands roamed over her body.

Her rhythm faltered. Suddenly, his arm was tightening around her waist, pulling her back to him even as his other hand gently squeezed her neck. Then he was thrusting up into her until the only thing she could concentrate on was the way her body turned in on itself as she got too close to the orgasm to hold it off.

"Let go for me, Boo," he whispered against her ear, running his hand down the column of her throat and across her chest before settling on holding onto her waist so both of his hands anchored her there as he thrust frantically into her. She couldn't stop her toes from curling, moans from starting and dying in her throat, or her eyes from fluttering closed before she forced them open so she could take in the sight of Zeke ramming into her. Zeke's head tipped back while he told her how good her pussy felt, how he'd always known she'd feel like heaven, and how he'd been waiting for her *for a long fucking time*. She clenched around him each time his rough, hoarse words hit the part of her that got off on how much he was enjoying this...but it was second to the pleasure that he built inside her with each thrust, each touch, each trail of his lips across her neck.

When Piper forced her eyes open and found Zeke staring at their reflections with the same lust-drunk look she had on her face, her body plummeted over the edge she'd been hanging onto for so long. The scream ripped through her throat even as all her nerve endings imploded. Shockwaves of pleasure still shot through her body as Zeke helped her off him. Her ass barely hit the chaise before he stood, his dick still impossibly hard, and hoisted her into the air.

He crossed the distance between the chaise and the bed in what felt like two large strides, placing her in the middle before crawling back up her body, trailing light kisses across her sweat-sheened skin as he went along. He didn't have to nudge her legs apart — they opened wantonly and greedily on their own. He swallowed her moans with a kiss as he entered her again with a smooth, deep thrust.

He brought his forehead to hers in a gesture so soft and intimate that Piper's heart tripped over itself for a quick second before she started regaining control of her emotions.

But when he brought his lips to hers again and whispered, "This is what dreams are made of," Piper knew she'd never be in control again.

fourteen

. . .

HE WAS GOING to take his time with her.

Oh, yes, he'd needed that first round...the unfettered lust, the images of the reflection of his dick sliding in and out of her, the sounds she made as his thrusts became harder and faster. He'd needed to take the edge off to break through the labyrinth of the desire — *need* — he had for her. He'd needed a head start on fucking Piper so he could be patient enough to do *this*.

Piper would never be his, but in this moment, on a California king bed with the moon high in the sky, Zeke intended to make love to her like she was.

He kept his thrusts deep but slow, languid even, as he tried to imprint in his mind the softness of Piper's skin under his fingertips and lips as he trailed kisses against her forehead, temple, and cheekbones before he reached the mouth he loved so much. God, he loved kissing Piper. They kissed like they'd been doing it for years, anticipating whether the other wanted gentle explorations of lips upon lips or the passionate dance of tongues lashing, teeth nipping until they struggled to catch a breath.

"Zeke," she moaned on a fluttering breath when he started punctuating each thrust with little circles. He took note of her reaction and continued it, even as his pace picked up a bit. Fast and hot sex was amazing, but there was something to be said about the slow burn of languid strokes, fingertips trailing over skin, deep kisses and foreheads pressed together as the burning deep inside grew from a simple spark to a raging inferno that spurred him to pick up the pace, to thrust harder.

He held her so close that her nipples slid against his chest each time he moved, and he could feel the vibration of the small mewling sounds she made. Piper wrapped her legs around his waist as her hands came to the back of his head and pulled him closer as her lips sought his. He kept up the slow march toward the orgasm that felt like it had been brewing for over a decade, groaning each time he felt Piper clenching around him.

"Look at me, baby," he whispered. "Please... I want to see your eyes when I come."

She caught his gaze and held it, pulling her lips between her teeth as Zeke struggled to keep his rhythm slow and steady. The pleasure built gradually, then so quickly that he was breathless as he got swept up in the wave. He came with Piper's name on his lips and her fingernails scratching his back as she cried out when her own orgasm pummeled into her.

He wasn't sure how long they lay there with their hearts beating erratically, Piper holding onto him tightly even though he was afraid he was suffocating her with his weight. "Wow," he whispered when he finally found his voice.

She rewarded him with a smile that was filled with as much satisfaction as it was mischief when she demanded, "Again."

fifteen

. . .

THE SUNLIGHT FILTERING in through the balcony doors hit Zeke's sleeping profile just right. Piper couldn't take her eyes off him. She'd been up for nearly twenty minutes, trying to get a grip on all the thoughts and emotions that pummeled into her as soon as she awoke with the steady sound of his heart beating against her ear.

She moved slowly, careful not to wake him when she slid out of his embrace and propped herself up on her elbow so she could watch him. He looked so calm and peaceful with the lips that had pulled pleasure from her just hours before settled into an adorable ass pout. She immediately craved a taste of him but managed, just barely, to resist leaning forward and brushing her lips against his.

Piper couldn't pull her eyes away from Zeke. All the features she should be— *was* — familiar with seemed different now, like she was looking at an entirely different person. Familiar, but strange...as if she was seeing him for the first time. Her heart tightened in her chest. She really couldn't perceive the Zeke she'd known all her life as the man who slept comfortably in their bed. She couldn't perceive him as the insufferable little brat who always seemed to get her and Angie into trouble, the awkward pre-teen who always seemed to trip over his words around her, or the popular, self-assured teenager with the range of inter-ests and mile-long list of plans for his life. She couldn't perceive him as the young adult she was surprised to find shared a lot of her interests and enjoyed the odd catch-up with every couple of months. Zeke almost seemed to trans-form into somebody else the night of his thirtieth birthday dinner, and she'd suddenly seen him as he was — confident, successful, and sexy as hell. Now, when she looked at him, all she could think about was the feel of his lips against hers, his fingers moving against her skin, and what it felt like to have him inside her. She would never be able to look at his smirk without thinking about the self-satisfied grins that graced his face when he knew he was driving her wild with pleasure. How would she ever be able to listen to him speak without remembering the shivers that swept down her spine when he whispered the most beautifully filthy things in her ear?

Her pussy pulsed with desire, and she briefly contem-plating pulling the covers back and waking him up with her mouth. That she still wanted him so badly surprised her. She didn't even know what time they eventually settled to sleep. Zeke told her he was going to give her everything she deserved on this trip, and apparently, he thought she deserved round after round of toe-curling, soul-shattering sex. She blushed when she thoughts of some of the things they did. She was pretty sure they'd defied the laws of physics and maybe a bit of biology, too.

She eased out of the bed, knowing if she stayed there any longer, she wouldn't be able to resist waking Zeke up so he could help soothe the ache deep inside her. And as satisfying as she knew that would be, Piper needed to gather her thoughts.

She found a branded hotel robe. Coffee called her name, but she didn't want to risk waking Zeke up by starting the machine, so she grabbed a bottle of water and made her way to the balcony.

The view of blue waters and sunshine sparkling like crystals against the ocean didn't do anything to ease the disquiet she felt. She'd been prepared for so many emotions when she woke up, primarily guilt for all the things she'd done with her best friend's little brother. But it wasn't guilt that left her feeling unsettled and restless. It was the pang of emotion that flooded her body when she first awoke with Zeke's arms wrapped around her and she nestled deeper into the warmth of his skin. It was the way her mind wandered, trying to imagine what it would be like to wake up with him, like this, every morning. It was how she was damn well near imagining a morning routine before she snapped out of it and pushed the reckless thoughts away. What good was it to fantasize about things that would not come to pass? *Could not.* The disappointment hit her as hard and fast as a sucker punch and almost left her gasping for breath.

"What have you gotten yourself into?" she whispered. It was bad enough that she wanted Zeke physically, that her body craved him like he was its own special drug. But the emotions threatening to push through... The tenderness? The giddiness? The way being around him just made her feel...*light*? Those were a different type of danger, and Piper feared she was fighting a losing battle even though the trip had barely begun.

She was still lost in her thoughts when Zeke stepped out on the balcony. He still looked a bit sleepy and had pulled on the sweatpants he'd worn the night before. She tried to avert her eyes from the dickprint in his loungewear, but his smirk let her know he'd caught her looking.

"Morning, baby," he said, and Piper's heart flipped in her chest. She hadn't been prepared for Zeke's voice tinged with sleep, or the way he looked at her as he settled into the wicker chair next to hers and intertwined their hands. She'd just about recovered from that when he leaned over and kissed her temple. "I woke up and missed you. It was nice falling asleep with you in my arms."

Please don't say that, her mind begged, but she couldn't make her mouth form the words. It was embarrassing how something inside her preened at the thought of him waking up to an empty bed and immediately coming in search of her. She could feel her mind wandering down hallways it had no business going, so she tried to change the topic. "Are you hungry?"

He nodded. "Starving."

Piper smiled. She could relate. They burned a lot of energy the night before.

"Okay, let's get ready for breakfast."

Zeke got up and helped her from the chair. She had just stepped into the room when he grabbed her by the waist and turned her around so he could press his lips to hers. He kissed her lazily for a few seconds before saying, "We can get ready for breakfast after."

"After what?"

"After I feast on what I really want to eat."

She'd barely comprehended his words before he was guiding her to the bed, opening her robe and running his hands all over her body until she was arching up toward him, hot and desperate for his touch. Then he spread her legs apart and pleasured her until her cries rang out in the room, until she was convinced that he could truly get sustenance from her body.

He grinned at her when she finally came down from an orgasm that had her gripping his head and bucking against him.

"Now we can go get breakfast."

sixteen

. . .

ZEKE GRABBED a can of Coke from the mini fridge and made his way to the balcony to wait for Piper to finish getting ready for the party that was currently going on at the main pool.

He leaned against the railing, too lost in thought to even contemplate the way the sky held a burst of orange as the sun set.

How do I come back from this?

He'd been asking himself that question for most of the day and was yet to come up with an answer.

He'd been naïve...arrogant, even...to think he could move through the weekend only concerned with sexual things. And although sex with Piper was easily the best sex he'd had in his entire life, the connection he felt with her was what had him wincing when he thought about how hard it was going to be to put the weekend behind him. Piper might not forget how it felt to have him make love to her like nothing else in the world mattered, but he would never forget how it felt in those moments, though brief, to know what it might feel like if Piper was *his*.

They'd spent most of the day walking hand in hand throughout the resort, completing a Halloween-themed scavenger hunt. He was surprised by how fun it was to explore the hotel while trying to decipher clues like *'This cursed object leaves its victim with seven days to live in the 2002 movie starring Naomi Watts,'* which had them sprinting to the TV lounge in search of a VHS containing the next clue. Piper raced through the scavenger hunt, brown eyes sparkling with an excitement that shimmered all around her. Zeke found himself just staring at her, captivated by her laughter, her beautiful smile, her excitement... her *essence*.

They completed the scavenger hunt before lunch time and were grabbing food in the hotel's main restaurant when they ran into Georgetta and Genae. Finding a table overlooking the pool that could comfortably fit four people, they sat with their plates and caught up on each pair's progress with the event. Genae turned to Piper with a smile on her face once the scavenger hunt conversation came to an end.

"You certainly look more relaxed," she said with a chuckle. He wondered if Piper realized how her gaze flicked to him before she grinned back at Genae, who'd started digging into her dessert, and said, "I don't know about relaxed, but I'm definitely rejuvenated."

The conversation turned to other things like the costumes they'd brought for the party the next night and how the sisters spent their night before Genae said she wanted to spend a few hours in San Jose del Cabo before returning for the pool party because it was a travesty she'd been to Cabo San Lucas nearly five times and hadn't made it out of Los Cabos.

That was how he and Piper ended up walking down cobbled streets, gentle breezes kissing their skin and the sun shining overhead. Piper was enthralled by the stores with all of their colorful wares, picking up a few souvenirs here and there before they popped into a small brewery to test the local beers.

Zeke was enthralled by her.

He was enthralled by the way her bright orange sundress fit her body and how easily she'd made friends with Georgetta and Genae, laughing conspiratorially when Georgetta mused the enchilada she'd had for lunch was better than her last three orgasms combined.

He was enthralled by how easily she leaned into him and reached for his hand, turned her chin up for a kiss, let him hold her and run his lips along her cheeks, and by how she hadn't corrected Genae when she gushed over how cute they were together. In those moments, it felt like they were just a couple hanging out with friends, and Zeke didn't want it to end.

Now, as he sat on the balcony and watched the sun set, Zeke realized how far he'd fallen. He'd spent so much of his life believing what he felt for Piper was just some byproduct of a teenage crush, a residual effect. But he'd been wrong. These feelings he had were wholly adult and *real*. Over the years he'd seen Piper from all angles — the good, the bad, and in between — and he'd found her beautiful from every point of view. This weekend was only confirming that he could love Piper...truly love her. And perhaps he already did.

He scrubbed a hand over his face before he returned to the room just as Piper was shrugging into her cover up, a gauzy, see-through material that perfectly showcased the tiny oxblood bikini she wore underneath.

"You're gorgeous," he whispered, smiling when she preened under the compliment, reaching up to him and pressing her lips against his.

"You ready?"

He nodded, falling behind as she made her way out of the room, always appreciating the view.

Piper was going to break his heart, tear it right open, and Zeke was realizing there wasn't a damn thing he could do about it.

He was going to allow her to. Because throwing up walls would mean he wouldn't experience *this*...whatever *this* was fully. The heartbreak would be a fair exchange for these few days where Piper felt like his, where she reached for his hand easily like she'd been doing it her whole life, where she leaned into him whenever she laughed, brushed her feet against his under tables, and fell asleep in his arms.

He'd navigate the heartbreak...eventually.

But for now, he would enjoy every single second of loving on Piper because he was almost running out of time.

seventeen

. . .

PIPER RAISED her hands above her head, stretching out the last remnants of sleep. She stifled a yawn with the palm of her hand before she finally sat up. Zeke's side of the bed was empty, but he'd sent a message to let her know he'd gone to check out the hotel's gym. She'd made a face when she read it because she couldn't figure out where he found the energy for a workout after the night before.

The pool party had been some of the most fun Piper had in a while. It was impeccably themed with the pool glowing red, a list of specialty cocktails and shots, and a truly elite Halloween hip-hop playlist. The DJ went from playing the slowed down, creepy version of "I Got 5 On It" by Luniz as it was styled for Jordan Peele's *Us* to Rihanna's "Disturbia" before moving smoothly into songs like Michael Jackson's "Thriller" — which had Zeke and a few other guys trying to do the dance in the pool — and rounding out the session with both the Ray Parker Jr. and Run-D.M.C versions of "Ghost-busters" playing. If anybody had told Piper that they'd be able to keep such a fun ass vibe going with just Halloween-themed songs, she wouldn't have believed it. She'd had so much fun dancing, drinking, and singing at the top of her lungs that she hadn't even realized when Saturday rolled over into Sunday and it was officially her birthday until Zeke grabbed her and spun her around, mouthing, "Happy Birthday, baby," before crashing his lips to hers for a kiss that left her body buzzing with anticipation that lasted even as they joined a few of the partygoers in taking Toxic Ooze shots in honor of her birthday.

The party was fun until the need for Zeke that had been buzzing under her skin became impossible to ignore, especially with the way he kept her pressed against him, hands caressing her skin as they danced in the water. She'd shifted in his arms so she could spin around and face him. "Let's get out of here."

She had sworn the night before couldn't be replicated — that perhaps it was the newness of his touch, his kisses, of *him* which made their coming together as intense as it was. But Piper was wrong. She started her birthday with lovemaking that felt like actual fireworks, and when it was all over, she fell asleep in the arms of a man she had no business falling for but had fallen anyway. Even if she didn't do a single thing else, this birthday had already shaped up to be one of the most satisfying she'd ever had, and she still had the Maleficent costume she'd been dying to wear tucked in her suitcase ahead of the costume party later that evening.

Piper quickly read and responded to the birthday greetings various people sent her and had just finished a telephone call with her parents, Sheila and Gordon, when a notification came in, letting her know that Angie wanted to video call. She answered with a broad smile on her face when her friend launched into her usual medley of the traditional "Happy Birthday" song followed by Stevie Wonder's version. Angie was always vaguely out of tune, but she sang with such gusto that Piper looked forward to her goofy birthday calls each year.

"Thank you," Piper said. "You're a little more on tune every year, so I know by my fiftieth you're going to be bang on."

Angie laughed. "Just for that, I'm not giving you the gift I got for you."

They joked back and forth for a few minutes before Piper updated her on her plans for the day. She was going to make use of the spa certificates she won during the Halloween trivia contest to get a full body massage, a facial, and use the hydrotherapy suite. She planned to spend the rest of the day lounging by the pool until it was time to get ready for the costume party. Angie made her promise to send photos before she ended the call just as Zeke returned to the room.

Piper couldn't stop the huge smile from spreading across her face at the sight of the huge bouquet of roses and bottle of champagne he had in his hands.

"The gym, huh?"

Zeke smiled, moving to the bed and handing her the bouquet. He pressed a kiss to her forehead before he pulled away. "I needed to explain my absence. I can't believe you fell for it, considering how much you wore me out last night."

"Pot, meet kettle." She chuckled, burying her face into the roses. The flowers were a nice surprise, and so was the glass of champagne he poured and handed to her. She was sipping on it when he disappeared for a few seconds and returned with a neatly wrapped box. It was covered in shiny pink paper, Piper's favorite color.

"When did you get this?" Piper asked. He hadn't been gone *that* long.

He smiled. "I packed it in my carry-on."

"When did you find the time to buy this? I don't even understand, you had less than a day to prepare for this trip."

"Open it," he said, bypassing her question altogether. He sat on the bed and pulled her legs across his. "I hope you like it."

She took her time unwrapping the box, finding that underneath, it was wrapped again in white paper, an emblem stamped in the red wax seal. Her eyes widened as she recognized it. "Zeke."

He nudged her. "Open your gift, Boo."

Her hands shook a little as she ripped off the white wrapping to reveal the red box she knew lay underneath. She flipped it open and stared.

Piper had been in love with watches for as long as she could remember, refusing to wear a smartwatch in favor of traditional timepieces. Hell, Aldis Hodge was her favorite actor just because he was into horology.

She'd been coveting a Pasha de Cartier for a while now, but she was a practical person, and dropping thousands of dollars on a watch when her teacher's salary already left a lot to be desired was not practical. So, she'd gotten a good dupe online and continued with her life.

"Zeke?" she asked, unable to keep the confusion from her voice. She lifted the watch from the box, admiring the rose gold and steel link bracelet and the rose gold bezel. The blue steel diamond-shaped hands were just as beautiful as she'd imagined they would be. Zeke reached forward and gently pulled back the crown cap to reveal that it was engraved simply with *Boo*. Piper's mouth dropped open as tears formed in her eyes. This wasn't a last-minute gift.

"When did you buy this? How did you buy this? Why did you buy—"

He silenced her with a short, sweet kiss. "Do you like it?"

"Like it?" she said. "That's an understatement, but Zeke, this is expensive."

He chuckled. "I know."

Questions still shot through her mind at lightning speed, but she settled on the most pressing one. "How did you know I wanted one of these?"

"You told me," he said simply. "A couple years ago, I think? You brought me some soup when I had the flu, and I convinced you to stay and watch *The Price is Right*. A smartwatch was an item during one of the mini games, and you went on the cutest rant about how technology was ruining the watch industry. We argued about the practical features of a smartwatch, and you said everything didn't have to serve a practical purpose. You got this wistful look on your face as you told me that owning expensive watches would always be your little impractical dream, so I asked you to show me the first one you'd buy if you had the money. That's when I decided I would get it for you. But every year, I stopped myself because I couldn't imagine giving you a gift like this without my feelings being obvious."

She was silent for a few seconds, allowing the words to wash over her. "When did you get this?"

That small smile that revealed his dimples she loved so much came out to play. "Shortly after we kissed. I hadn't expected you to go ghost on me and I figured we'd have to talk about it eventually. Once the cat was out of the bag, there wouldn't be anything stopping me from giving you a gift I knew you'd love."

He took the watch from her hands. "Ready to put it on?"

Piper took a deep breath, shocked by how feeling his touch against her skin sent her body and her emotions into overdrive as he clasped it on her wrist. She looked at the watch, running her fingertips along the rose gold bezel before bringing her gaze back to Zeke and found him smiling at her.

"It comes with an alternate leather band. I know you love pink, but I chose the blue one because I figured you'd love the way it went with the hands," he said.

"I don't know what to say," she said.

"I accept gratitude in kisses."

"Oh, that I can do," she whispered, bringing her lips to his. She immediately sank into the kiss. If this was the way he wanted to be thanked, she was willing to thank him until the end of time.

He pulled away far more quickly than Piper liked. "As much as I'd like to follow this kiss to its natural conclusion, they're coming to set up breakfast on the balcony in a few min—"

He hadn't even finished the sentence before a few knocks sounded against the door. He kissed her forehead and pushed himself up off the bed. "Let's get this party started."

Then he wandered off to open the door, leaving her staring at him, at her watch, and at the flowers on the bed, wondering if she was still asleep. Because it sure as hell seemed like she'd dreamed up her perfect man. Except he wasn't hers. And he could never be.

Piper fought the dark feelings that rose within her. She put on a winning smile when room service came into the room and headed out to the balcony. They had a final night, and she wouldn't ruin it with unrealistic dreams. She had him now, and that was going to have to be enough.

eighteen

. . .

PIPER TRIED to swallow her moan, but it escaped as a small, keening sob when Zeke interlaced his hand with hers as he continued his deep, slow strokes. Each time she convinced herself it couldn't get any more pleasurable, that he couldn't take her any higher, that she couldn't want him more...*it* did. *She* did.

It wasn't lost on her that she was in the exact position she'd fantasized about being in during Zeke's birthday dinner — flat on her back, legs on his shoulders, and his gold chain dangling in her face.

It was a shame she hadn't accounted for the tender feelings that filled her chest.

The feelings that were there while they ate her birthday breakfast on the balcony, toasting with the champagne as they enjoyed the view and conversation.

The feelings that were there when he reached out and held her hand as they got settled on massage beds for their couples massage.

The feelings that were there while they lounged poolside with their e-readers, reading silently as they sipped on cocktails with the occasional bout of public display of affection steamy enough to make other guests avert their gaze.

The feelings that were there when she got the first glimpse of his Blade costume, convinced he was going to be the sexiest man at the party. And she wasn't wrong.

The feelings that were there as she watched him mingling with the other guests and his easy affection for Georgette and Genae, ensuring that they too never had an empty cup in their hands and that they were enjoying the party.

He'd been pulled aside to take photos with a man dressed up as Van Helsing when Genae, who was dressed as Storm, pulled her aside and said, "I mean this in the most respectful way but…damn, your man. Sexy, smart, and sweet enough to give a girl cavities. The Universe was smiling down on you."

She'd fixed her mouth to explain that Zeke wasn't her boyfriend, but she stopped herself. For these moments, she basked in a reality that could not exist and instead said to Genae, "You haven't said a wrong thing yet."

She didn't even make it halfway through the costume party, not even to the announcement of the best costumes, before she was feigning a headache, saying her goodbyes to her friends, and dragging Zeke off to the room, where she allowed herself a slow exploration of his body, wanting to commit it to memory for the nights when she ached for him. She took him in her mouth and pleased him until he shattered, coating her tongue with his release, and she gladly swallowed it all.

And now she was here, heart in her throat as they climbed that crest together, his slow, deep thrusts becoming faster and more insistent until they were both crying out and screaming each other's names while their bodies shook.

Long after it was over, she snuggled into Zeke, relaxing against his steady breathing. The countdown to the end of the trip was as loud as the blaring horn of a train in her head. She didn't want to go home. Not yet. She didn't want reality to catch up to them. But reality couldn't be avoided, nor could it be outrun. It would catch up with them, whether Piper wanted it to or not.

nineteen

. . .

REALITY WAS WORSE than Zeke imagined.

He hadn't been prepared for the angst that pressed against his chest as he made the sweetest love to Piper right before it was time to check out of the hotel.

Reality was more than a sucker punch, it was a fucking knockout as they stumbled through their final breakfast together, neither wanting to address the elephant in the room. And maybe that was for the best. Maybe then, they would have been able to enjoy the outdoor seating next to the pool with the blue sky overhead and faint sounds of classical music playing. But Zeke didn't know how to leave good and well enough alone.

"Boo?"

He caught her mid-sip of her morning coffee. He wasn't sure if it was the look on his face or the hesitancy in his voice, but it seemed as if Piper instantly knew what he wanted to address.

"The one thing this resort hasn't managed to get right is its coffee," she said, voice slightly tremulous and eyes pleading with him to drop whatever he was going to say. But Zeke couldn't. Maybe it was because his feelings for her had been a secret he believed destined to die on his tongue. Maybe it was because he couldn't see that he had anything left to lose. He couldn't deny the obvious any longer, and he knew from the way Piper refused to meet his eyes that she couldn't deny what was clear for her to see, either. Then there was the small matter that every interaction they'd had this weekend made him suspect she was feeling some of the things he felt too.

"We're good together," he said. "I know you see it. I know you *feel* it. I've spent so many years telling myself what I felt whenever I was near to you was a lingering effect of the silly little crush I had as a kid, but I know better now. Being with you is simultaneously everything I've ever dreamed it to be and surpasses everything I thought was possible."

"Zeke…"

"Let me get this off my chest, Boo. I don't know exactly what I expected to come out of this weekend, but damn it, Piper, all it's done is reaffirm what I've known to be true. Nobody can make me feel the way you do, and we're so fucking good together."

She fixed him with a small, sad smile that crushed his heart. "We can't be together for real, you know…"

She allowed the words to trail off as if she couldn't think of anything she wanted less than saying them.

"I know what?"

"We can't…"

"I'm just asking you to see where this can go. Nothing more, nothing less. I think we owe it to ourselves."

"We can't."

"Tell me you don't think we're good together," he said. "Tell me that *that* is why you don't want to try and I'll dead this right now."

Zeke watched the myriad of emotions dance across Piper's

face but couldn't even find satisfaction in knowing she wasn't able to tell him that. She settled on annoyance, doing the most predictably Piper thing by reaching for anger instead of being vulnerable.

"I don't know what to say to you. I already told you that this weekend was all I could offer. You have no right to switch up on me now."

He bit back the snarky comment that rose to his lips because she was right. He sighed. "I'm sorry. You're right."

"Zeke…" Her voice was softer now, but he didn't want to hear what she had to say. He reached across the table to cover her hand with his and squeezed.

"Forget I ever said anything. Let's enjoy our last few hours here. When we get home, it'll be like none of this ever happened."

twenty

. . .

One Month Later

IT'LL BE *like none of this ever happened.*

Piper couldn't forget the look on Zeke's face when he spoke those words the day they left Mexico a little over a month ago. His expression was vacant, but she knew it was because he was trying to hide how he truly felt, which she was sure was something akin to devastation — because she felt it too. Along with guilt, because she was the one who made the decision…she was the one who denied them even a chance. She'd wanted to find the words to show him things from her perspective. She wanted him to see that she was scared, that she was unwilling to risk the dynamic of her friendship with Angie and her closeness with their family because there was no coming back if things ended badly. In the end, she remained silent. Her emotions were an erratic mess because she had no business feeling anger at Zeke's words when that was what she'd been asking for all along.

Piper had expected the weeks to dull the sadness and frustration she felt, but time just made things worse.

When she was with Zeke for those three days, she felt the little click, the rightness, the fullness in her heart that she'd trying to find for years. She'd searched for it in men she met in bars, in cafés, on dating apps, and even this one man she shared a yellow cab with on a rainy afternoon. She'd become jaded after a while, convinced she'd never find it. And then she went ahead and found it with her best friend's little brother. But she couldn't imagine it being anybody other than Zeke. No matter how hard she tried, how badly she wanted it to be *like none of this ever happened*, she couldn't push her memories or her feelings for Zeke from her mind.

She could not forget.

And god knows she tried.

Yet, she remembered the exact pressure and movement of his lips against her mouth and across skin that burned for him. She remembered those lips moving expertly against her center, pulling pleasure from her until lights erupted behind her eyelids. She remembered how her hand felt in his…like it belonged there. She remembered how it felt to be sat on his lap, his arms around her waist and his chin resting on her shoulder, and she embraced how much he'd felt like *home*.

She couldn't forget his thoughtfulness, not with her watch resting against her wrist and the memories of how in tune he'd been with her every single need. How bringing a smile to her face seemed like his sole mission in life.

Her heart hurt when she remembered his smile, the very particular smile that seemed reserved only for her — a smile that, looking back, she realized he'd had forever. A smile she'd ached for during the awkward Thanksgiving meal that still made her skin itch with embarrassment even a week later.

Piper was miserable. She was in her feelings, and she was starting to think she'd need an excavator to get herself out. She sat in her apartment, the TV playing a show she wasn't paying attention to and a new novel open but unread. She'd been halfway through her second bag of Cheetos when her phone chimed with an incoming message from Angie.

ANG

SOS. Tremaine got called out to work and I'm bored out my mind. Come watch a movie with me? I'll send a rideshare.

Piper resisted the urge to feign exhaustion or busyness. She was sitting at home being a miserable mess, captive to thoughts which were starting to move into uncomfortable territory.

Am I a coward?

Did I make a mistake?

Will I regret this forever?

An overdue chill session with Angie was probably just what she needed. A reminder of what she didn't want to risk by trying to explore her feelings for Zeke. Decision made, she quickly composed a reply.

PIPER

See you soon!

twenty-one

· · ·

PIPER'S EMOTIONS were more evenly keeled by the time she let herself into Angie's Brooklyn apartment a few hours later.

She'd expected to find her friend lounging on the couch, but she found her in the kitchen, standing in her walking boot. Angie was busy setting up a charcuterie board, slicing and plating cheese while the sultry tones of Ari Lennox filled the apartment, dressed casually in white silk pajamas with her box braids pulled back from her face. She looked up when she heard Piper enter and smiled.

Piper's heart stuttered in her chest. *Holy shit.* She hadn't realized how alike Angie's and Zeke's smiles were until that very moment. The commitment she'd made to not think about Zeke during the pep talk she gave herself on the cab ride over fled, and she was immediately left with an aching in her chest. She forced herself to move forward, plastering a smile on her face as she enveloped Angie in a hug and stole a cube of sharp cheddar from the board. It wasn't lost on her that the month before, she'd been in this very apartment trying to hide her feelings from Angie, and she was about to do it again.

They chitchatted while Angie finished the spread before moving to the living room with a bottle of white wine. They ate in silence, Angie making no move to turn on the TV or showing any indication she planned to watch a movie. She just kept topping her crackers with cheese and cold cuts and sipping wine until she abruptly looked at Piper and said, "So…you and Zeke, huh?"

Everything slowed down as Piper tried to focus on swallowing what was in her mouth without choking.

"Excuse me?" she said after a few seconds, her voice a bit too squeaky and a bit too guilty to be fooling anybody, least of all Angie. Her mind went at a hundred miles per hour as she watched her best friend tilt her head to the side and raise an eyebrow.

"I think you heard me just fine."

"Did Zeke talk to you?" she asked, but even as the words came out of her mouth, she knew it couldn't be true. Zeke wouldn't have betrayed her confidence, not even while he was hurt and disappointed.

Angie made a face. "Piper, my leg's broken, not my brain. Who do you think was buying that excuse you came up with for the one bed in the room? Not to mention when I called you for your birthday, there was *still* only one bed. Lie to somebody else."

Piper didn't say anything. She couldn't say anything, not when embarrassment was creeping up her spine. She took a good look at her best friend. She didn't look angry, annoyed, or even particularly bothered.

"I can explain."

Angie raised her hand, palm facing out. "Sis, I love you, but I do not want to hear any explanation that might get a mile within forcing me to confront Zeke's sex life. I just want to know why things are so weird between you two. Thanksgiving was so tense I considered hobbling out the door just to escape all the tension radiating off you and the puppy dog looks Zeke kept flinging in your direction when he thought nobody was looking. I've been waiting for you to confide in me about whatever is going on, but clearly, you don't plan to."

Piper couldn't miss the hurt in her voice this time around.

"I didn't want to upset you."

"Upset me?"

She sighed. "Yes. Zeke and I...got close in Cabo." She laughed despite the heaviness she felt when Angie made a face. "He wanted to see where things could go, but I told him I didn't want to make things awkward with you, so we should keep things as they are."

Angie's eyes widened. "Whoa, whoa! How did I get into this? You could've turned him down for so many reasons, but please keep me out of it. It's none of my business."

"Come on," Piper said. "He's your little brother..."

"And you're my best friend. You could've spoken to me, and I would have told you exactly this."

"Do you remember how you nearly dog-walked Melanie that one time she made a comment about how cute he was? That did not make me confident you'd embrace my feelings for Zeke."

A little smile tugged at Angie's face. "Your feelings for Zeke, huh? You in love with the brat or what?"

"Angie!"

Her best friend chuckled. "My reaction to Melanie might have been over the top, but firstly, he was only twenty-one then. He's a grown ass man now. And secondly, it was *Melanie*. I don't even want her around my food, much less my little brother. You and Melanie are not in the same category. Pleeease get a grip."

Piper laughed, feeling a bit of her tension drain away. They sat in comfortable silence for a few minutes before she asked, "So you wouldn't mind?"

Angie shrugged. "Would it take some getting used to? Yes. Would you ever be able to talk to me about your sex life? No. But yeah, I'm okay with it because it's not about me. It's about both of you, and when you decide what you want, I shouldn't be a factor *at all*."

She sat with that for a few moments, allowing hope to bloom in her chest.

"Piper?" Angie asked, her voice soft. "What do you want?"

"Zeke."

His name slipped from her lips without a moment's hesitation. She hadn't wanted anything more completely than she did this.

"Well," Angie said, a huge smile spreading across her face. "I think you should go get your man."

twenty-two

. . .

THE DOORBELL JOLTED ZEKE AWAKE, the book he had been reading falling to the carpeted floor. For a few seconds, he thought he'd conjured the noise in his sleep-addled brain, but then it rang again. He tried to rub the bleariness from his eyes. His phone glowed, announcing the time was ten-thirty p.m., and Zeke couldn't fathom who would be trying to get him at this time of night. He fully expected it to be a delivery person at the wrong address when he looked through the peephole, but he was greeted by the last person he expected to see.

The sight of Piper chased away the last remnants of sleep, leaving him confused but alert. She was fidgeting, continuously tucking loose strands of hair behind her ear and shifting her weight from one leg to the other. He opened the door, watching her gaze dip to his bare chest before returning to his eyes.

"Hey," she said. "Can I come in?"

He stepped back, allowing her into the apartment, trying his best to not stare at her. As disappointed as he was with the decision she'd made, he couldn't be angry at her, and he still thought she was the most beautiful woman in existence, even with the nervous energy that bounced off her.

"Are you okay?" he asked, concerned, wondering what had pushed her to come see him.

She started to answer, stopped…began to try again before she stopped once more. She gestured to the couch. "Can we sit?"

"Sure. Do you want something to drink? I've got sodas, juice, and maybe a few beers."

Piper shook her head, so he joined her on the couch, amazed that conversation could be so stilted between them. He waited.

"I spoke to Angie," she said. "Well, Angie spoke to me. She knows."

Everything clicked into place, and he was surprised by the slight bitterness he felt. "I didn't tell Angie about us."

He cringed. *Us.* There was no *us.* Piper had been abundantly clear.

"Oh, no," she said quickly, voice a little breathless. "I never once thought you had, not even while you're mad at me—"

"I'm not mad."

She shook her head with a small smile. "You are mad. Well, at least disappointed with the way I handled things. I guess I don't blame you. If it helps, I've been so miserable since we came back. Distraught, actually."

His laughter was without humor. "That doesn't help, but I guess there is comfort in solidarity because I've been miserable too."

A few beats of silence passed before she spoke again.

"Angie is the sister I never had. I got it into my head that she'd hate the idea of us together, and I didn't want to risk causing a rift in our friendship…or between you two. And I guess there was the part of me that was worried I was just something you needed to get out of your system, and then I might have ruined my friendship and get my heart broken too."

Zeke moved closer to Piper. He reached for her hands and was encouraged when she allowed him to hold them. Hope started to rise within him, but he pushed it down, not wanting to get his feelings crushed.

"You're not just something to get out of my system, Boo. You're not just a phase. I've never felt this way about anyone…"

A small smile tugged at lips he was desperate to kiss. "I don't think I've felt this way about anyone either."

"I still mean everything I said in Mexico," Zeke said, needing her to know nothing had changed. He still wanted her more than he'd ever wanted anything in his life, and he was willing to take things as quickly or as slowly as she was comfortable with.

"I want to be with you." She said it so quickly, it came out in one long breath. "I want to try…except I have no idea what any of that would look like."

Zeke smiled. The relief that rushed through him was forceful enough that he was almost dizzy. He brought his lips to hers for a kiss that she eagerly received. "We'll just take it one step at a time."

Piper nodded, and Zeke was happy to see some of the tension drain from her body. "I think I can do that."

"First step, you allow me to love you," he whispered against her lips. "Can you do that?"

"I can."

"And second step, you allow me to show you how much I missed you."

Piper giggled. "I can definitely do that."

Hours later, Zeke pulled a sleeping Piper into him, both

exhausted from the love they made. They reacquainted themselves with each other slowly, knowing there was no need to rush now. They'd have each other tomorrow and the day after and the day after that. He kissed her forehead, sinking into the complete contentment he felt in that moment. They would take things one step at a time while they found their footing, but Zeke didn't mind. Each step would lead to another, and eventually, all those steps would lead to what he really wanted from her. Forever. And Piper was more than worth the wait.

epilogue

. . .

Three Years Later

THEY CHOSE to get married on Halloween. Zeke had thrown out the date as a suggestion a few weeks after his proposal in Cancun. Even now, almost a year later, Piper's eyes still welled with tears when she remembered the ocean-front candlelit dinner which ended with Zeke down on one knee with a large marquise cut diamond in his hand and the sweetest words on his lips.

"I've spent over half of my life imagining what it would be like to be with you, and nothing I dreamed up came close to the magic of reality with you. Thank you for taking a chance on us. Thank you for giving me the opportunity to love you. It's been the greatest honor in my life. Will you give me the privilege of loving you forever?"

She swiped a teardrop from her eye, but not before Tallulah, the makeup artist who was dealing with Angie's makeup, spotted her and sighed. "You're putting all this makeup's claims of being waterproof to the test, sis."

Angie laughed. "Have faith in your products, Tallulah. It'll be okay. Besides, Zeke's so love-drunk that she could show up looking like a rain-soaked clown and he would sing praises to her beauty."

Piper laughed, her happiness bouncing off the walls of the bright, airy bridal suite of the Virginia vineyard they'd chosen as their wedding venue. "Angie! Stop."

Her best friend simply shrugged, eyes bright with mischief. "Tell me I'm wrong. Go 'head and lie to me. 'Lil brother's smitten…obsessed…gone…and all in capital letters!'"

Her voice turned soft and serious. "I'm so happy for y'all. It's been amazing watching your love bloom. And to think, I get to tell people I was the cause of it all."

"Well…not just you."

Angie rolled her eyes, pulling her black silk robe more tightly around her body. "I can't believe y'all put that damn cat in the ceremony."

"What can I say?" Piper teased. "We're a sentimental couple, and Finchly is an integral part of our origin story."

"You're lucky I love you both. Finchly better not cross me, though, because he'll be down two lives."

"I hope your in-laws don't hear the constant threats you keep leveling against their cat."

"Am I missing a story?" Tallulah asked, forehead crinkling in confusion. For the next thirty minutes, Piper and Angie filled Tallulah in on the beef between Angie and her husband's mother's cat and how it led to Piper and Zeke's eventual romance.

"That's one hell of a story," Tallulah said with a grin. She turned to Piper. "Come, let me touch up your makeup one last time. I've got a feeling you guys' next chapter is going to be stunning."

———

Stunning didn't come close to describing the beauty of Piper and Zeke's ceremony.

The vineyard had spectacular views of the Blue Ridge Mountains, and the sky had already started turning a vibrant shade of orange as the sun got ready to set when the wedding procession began. Piper waited in the wings, watching Angie walk down the aisle lined with miniature pumpkins carved with Zeke and Piper's names and their wedding date. The burnt orange dress looked amazing against her skin, and instead of a traditional bouquet, she held a tiny pumpkin filled with orange pansies. She kissed Zeke's cheek when she got to the top of the aisle and whispered something that made him throw his head back and laugh, and Piper almost started crying again. What a beautiful man. *Her* beautiful man.

Zeke's best friend Rayon went next, holding the infamous tabby cat in his arms. Finchly was dressed in a tiny tuxedo, and Piper grinned at the audible *awws* she heard from the wedding guests. Finchly looked adorable as hell, and Piper knew that even with her expert-level hating, Angie would have to admit it. He was so chilled out that nobody would believe the part he played in the Piper and Zeke's love story. He'd been chilled out all weekend, and Piper wasn't sure if it was just Finchly's normal personality when he wasn't committing acts of grievous bodily harm or if Tremaine had been dosing him with catnip. Tremaine refused to confirm or deny.

"Are you ready?"

Piper turned to her father with a huge smile, smoothing down the simple A-line ivory wedding dress she wore as she nodded. She'd never been more ready for anything in her life. And when Gordon held his hand out to her, leading her down the aisle, she kept her eyes fixed on the man who'd changed her life.

Who would have thought that a childhood crush, a cat, and an unexpected trip could have bloomed into something so beautiful?

She blinked back happy tears as, with slow steps, she moved closer to her forever.

"Hey, Boo," Zeke whispered, voice thick with emotion, reaching for her hands.

"My love," she said softly. "Ready?"

Zeke chuckled. "Only for about my entire life."

Then there, as the sun set, Zeke and Piper pledged to love and honor each other for the rest of their lives, and when the marriage officer finally gave them permission to kiss, Zeke pulled her in tight and kissed her until cheers rang up from their guests. He pulled away with a small smile on his face, gently stroking her cheek. "Loving you will continue to be the greatest adventure of my life."

He pressed his lips to hers. "I love you, Piper. My love. My life. My wife. Here's to forever."

She pulled him in by the lapels of his suit for another kiss that set the guests cheering. "And ever…and ever."

THE END

afterword

Thank you for taking this quick journey with Piper and Zeke.

If you liked this book, please think about rating it and/or leaving a review on Amazon and/or Goodreads and telling your friends about it. Word of mouth is so important for indie authors.

Peace. Love. Light.
Rilzy

acknowledgments

Brandon: Thank you for being super supportive, super sweet and always ready to validate my emotions when listening to me rant. You always believed in me when I was ready to give up and knew when to tell me I needed to rest and regroup at a later stage. You're the best! <3

Bre: Thanks for always listening and bribing me with sushi to start writing sessions.

Kaitesi: Another year of me putting you through it! I'm forever amazed at how you whip a manuscript into shape. It's almost like a magic trick. I cannot wait to see where the next year takes us.

To everyone who encouraged me to continue writing this book even though there was no way it would be ready in time for Halloween: THANK YOU!

about the author

Rilzy Adams is a lover of love and happily ever afters. She spends too much time living in her head watching the romantic lives of her 'imaginary friends' play out and then being the chatty friend to tell the world about them.

When she isn't living in her head, she must show up to work every day and be a lawyer.

She resides, with her two dogs, on an island in the middle of the Caribbean Sea, which is perfect for her sun addiction, love affair with Prosecco and sushi worship.

For information on new releases, promotions and more: Join the Mailing List.

Visit her website at: www.rilzywrites.com

also by rilzy adams